ANN M. MARTIN

THE BABY-SITTERS CLUB®

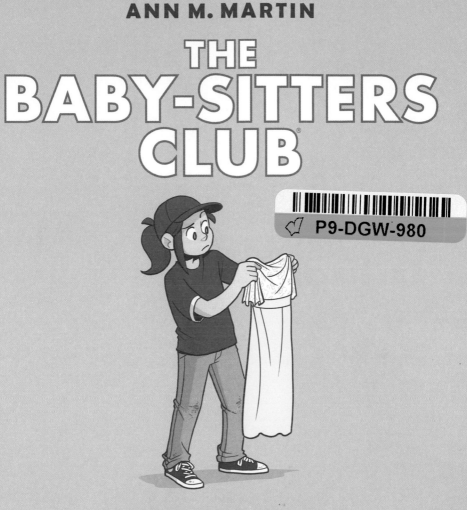

KRISTY'S BIG DAY

A GRAPHIC NOVEL BY

GALE GALLIGAN

WITH COLOR BY BRADEN LAMB

An Imprint of

SCHOLASTIC

Library of Congress Control Number: 2017955790

ISBN 978-1-338-06768-2 (hardcover)
ISBN 978-1-338-88828-7 (paperback)

10 9 8 7 6 5 4 3 2 1 23 24 25 26 27

Printed in China 62
This edition first printing, April 2023

Edited by Cassandra Pelham Fulton and David Levithan
Book design by Phil Falco
Creative Director: David Saylor

WELL, THIS IS IMPORTANT INFORMATION FOR YOU, KRISTY. WHEN YOU MOVE INTO OUR HOUSE, YOU'RE GOING TO WANT TO KNOW **EVERYTHING** ABOUT OUR GREAT-GRANDFATHER.
flop
ESPECIALLY IF YOU GET A BEDROOM ON THE **THIIIRD FLOOOOR.**
meep
I...I THINK THAT'S ENOUGH GHOST TALK FOR ONE DAY.
HI THERE.
I'M KRISTY THOMAS, AND THE CUTE KIDS YOU SEE HERE ARE KAREN AND ANDREW.
THEIR FATHER IS ENGAGED TO MY MOTHER. WHEN OUR PARENTS GET MARRIED, KAREN AND ANDREW WILL BECOME MY LITTLE STEPSISTER AND STEPBROTHER...
AND MY BROTHERS AND I WILL MOVE OUT OF THE HOUSE WHERE WE GREW UP, AND INTO WATSON'S **MANSION.**

CHAPTER 1

AND BEFORE THAT, THE MANSION BELONGED TO OLD BEN BREWER.

HE ATE FRIED DANDELIONS, AND AFTER HE TURNED FIFTY, HE NEVER LEFT HOME...
EXCEPT TO GO OUT IN THE YARD TO GET MORE DANDELIONS.

THEN HE DIED, AND HIS GHOST **STAYED IN OUR ATTIC.**

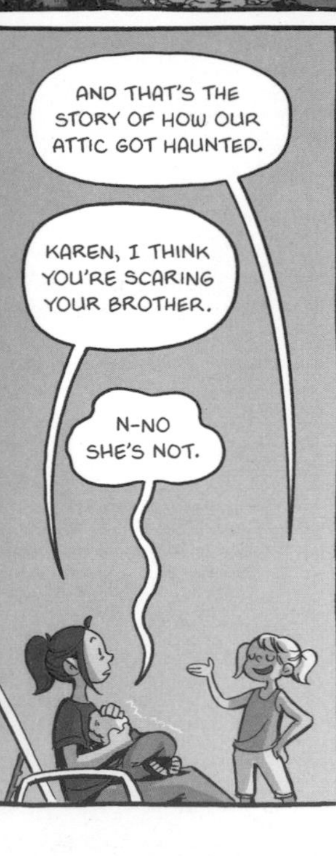

AND THAT'S THE STORY OF HOW OUR ATTIC GOT HAUNTED.
KAREN, I THINK YOU'RE SCARING YOUR BROTHER.
N-NO SHE'S NOT.

KRISTY THOMAS
PRESIDENT

CLAUDIA KISHI
VICE PRESIDENT

MARY ANNE SPIER
SECRETARY

STACEY MCGILL
TREASURER

DAWN SCHAFER
ALTERNATE OFFICER

MALLORY PIKE
JUNIOR OFFICER

For Max, William, Durinn, Nate, and Lily.

And for Patrick, who is much older than these
cool babies, but still manages to have a good time.

G. G.

THERE ARE PROS AND CONS. THE PROS: I WASN'T KIDDING ABOUT THE MANSION -- WATSON'S RICH. LIKE, **MILLIONAIRE-RICH.**

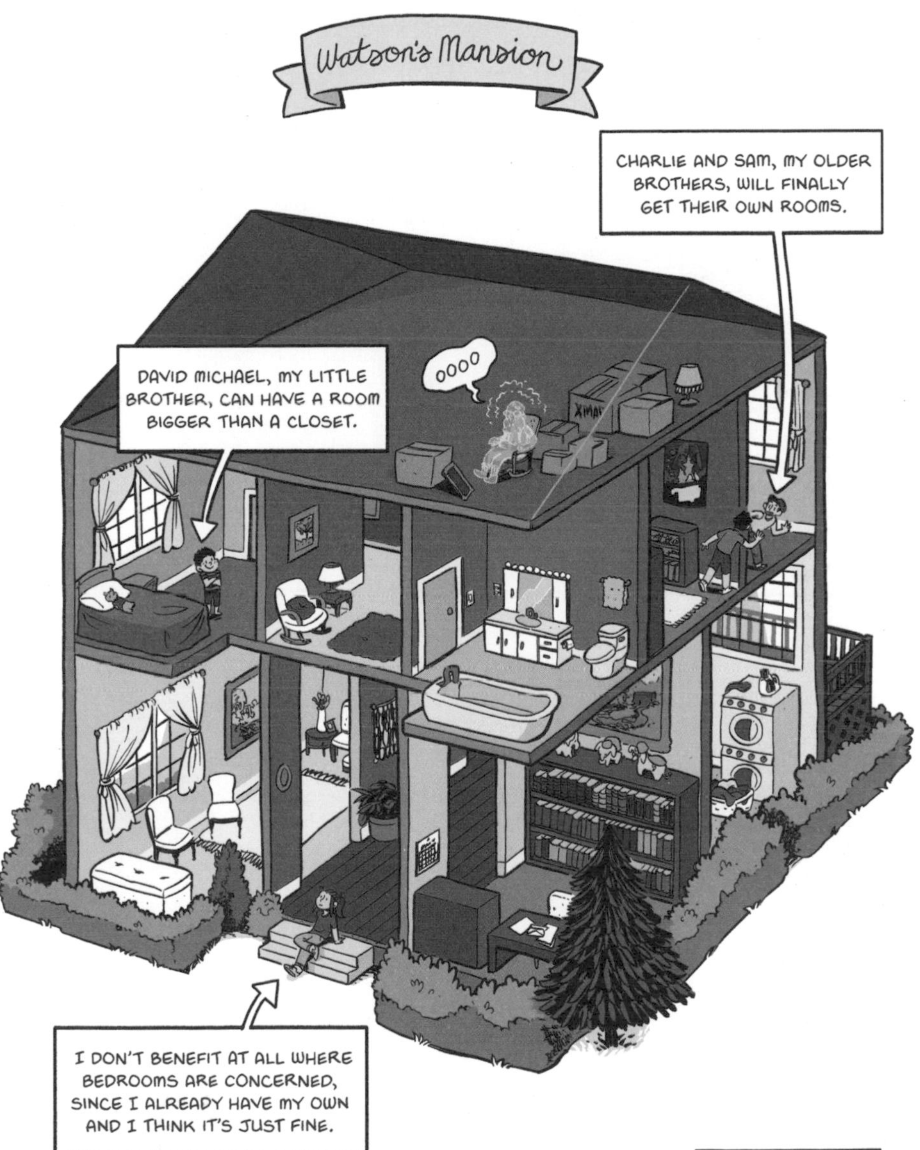

Watson's Mansion
CHARLIE AND SAM, MY OLDER BROTHERS, WILL FINALLY GET THEIR OWN ROOMS.
DAVID MICHAEL, MY LITTLE BROTHER, CAN HAVE A ROOM BIGGER THAN A CLOSET.
OOOO
I DON'T BENEFIT AT ALL WHERE BEDROOMS ARE CONCERNED, SINCE I ALREADY HAVE MY OWN AND I THINK IT'S JUST FINE.

WHAT'S THE **CON,** YOU ASK?

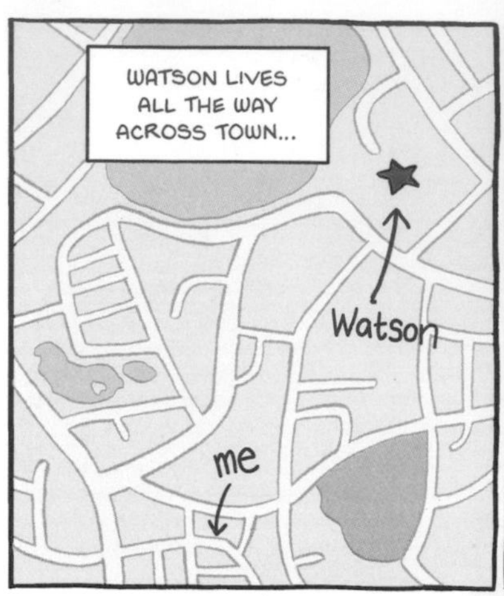

ALL MY FRIENDS ARE HERE. MY BEST FRIEND AND NEXT-DOOR NEIGHBOR, MARY ANNE SPIER... CLAUDIA KISHI RIGHT ACROSS THE STREET... STACEY MCGILL, DAWN SCHAFER, AND MALLORY PIKE JUST A FEW BLOCKS OVER.

THE SIX OF US MAKE UP **THE BABY-SITTERS CLUB...**

THIS LOOKS GREAT, MOM, BUT IT'S SO **NICE** OUT. SHOULDN'T WE EAT OUTSIDE?
SPAGHETTI IN OUR LAPS? THAT SOUNDS LIKE THE START OF A DETERGENT COMMERCIAL.

SPA-GHET-TI! SPA-GHET-TI!

I CAN'T BELIEVE WE'RE GONNA HAVE **FOUR** BROTHERS.
WE'D BETTER STICK TOGETHER.

I'LL HAVE **TWO SISTERS!**

IT'S WEIRD THINKING ABOUT HOW THINGS ARE GOING TO CHANGE AFTER THE WEDDING.

FOR EXAMPLE, MOM'S AFRAID THERE'S GOING TO BE TROUBLE BETWEEN KAREN AND DAVID MICHAEL. THEY'RE CLOSE ENOUGH IN AGE THAT THEY'RE PROBABLY GOING TO BE COMPETING FOR THINGS, LIKE TOYS AND PRIVILEGES.
HI, DAVID MICHAEL.
HEY.

NOT TO MENTION, KAREN GOES TO PRIVATE SCHOOL AND DAVID MICHAEL GOES TO PUBLIC SCHOOL, SO THEY MIGHT COMPARE THEMSELVES THAT WAY.

THEN THERE'S THE AGE STUFF. KAREN'S USED TO BEING THE OLDEST, AND DAVID MICHAEL'S USED TO BEING THE BABY, BUT WE'RE ALL GETTING MASHED TOGETHER.

AND GOODNESS KNOWS WHAT ANDREW THINKS.

WELL, WE'VE SET THE DATE.
WHAT DATE?
THE DATE OF THE **WEDDING!**
IT'LL BE THE THIRD SATURDAY IN SEPTEMBER.
UM.
WHAT'S A WEDDING?
YOU KNOW. I SHOWED YOU A WHOLE WEDDING.
REMEMBER WHEN I PUT ON THE LONG WHITE DRESS AND KISSED BOO-BOO?
BOO-BOO IS THE BREWERS' CAT.

WE'VE TALKED ABOUT THE WEDDING, ANDREW. AND EVERYONE HERE IS GOING TO BE A PART OF IT.
WE **ARE?**
IF YOU WANT TO BE.
KRISTY...
I'D LIKE YOU TO BE MY BRIDESMAID.

REALLY? LIKE IN A LONG, FANCY DRESS WITH FLOWERS IN MY HAIR?

SINCE WHEN DO YOU LIKE LONG FANCY DRESSES AND FLOWERS?
SINCE RIGHT NOW.

IS THAT A YES?
YOU'LL BE MY BRIDESMAID?

IT'S A YES-YES-YES!!

AND, CHARLIE, I'D BE HONORED IF YOU GAVE ME AWAY.
SURE.
SAM, I'D LIKE YOU TO BE MY BEST MAN.
AND DAVID MICHAEL WILL BE THE RING BEARER.
WHAT ABOUT ME?
HOW WOULD YOU LIKE TO BE OUR FLOWER GIRL? YOU'D WALK UP THE AISLE IN FRONT OF ELIZABETH AND ME, CARRYING A BASKET OF ROSE PETALS.
OOOOH.
AND ANDREW CAN ESCORT YOU. THAT MEANS HE'LL WALK BESIDE YOU.
I DON'T WANT TO BE IN THE WEDDING.
AND I MEAN IT.
WELL, THINK IT OVER. WE'D LIKE YOU TO BE IN THE WEDDING, BUT IT'S UP TO YOU, OKAY?
OKAY.

THE ONLY THING I COULD THINK ABOUT WAS THE WEDDING.

I, KRISTIN AMANDA THOMAS, WAS GOING TO BE A BRIDESMAID!

CHAPTER 2

I HAVE USUALLY FOUND THAT, IN LIFE, GOOD THINGS ARE FOLLOWED BY BAD THINGS.
ONE DAY, AN EXTRA SNACK FALLS FROM THE VENDING MACHINE, THE NEXT, IT EATS YOUR QUARTER.
A RUN OF GOOD LUCK IS FOLLOWED BY A RUN OF BAD LUCK.
IT WAS THAT WAY WITH THE WEDDING.
ON SATURDAY WE HAD ALL THAT GOOD NEWS.
click
THEN, JUST FOUR DAYS LATER...

MOM! YOU'RE HOME!
...ARE YOU SICK?
NO, HONEY, I'M FINE. BUT, WELL, I JUST CAN'T BELIEVE WHAT HAPPENED TODAY.
UH-OH.
FOR STARTERS, THE COMPANY WANTS TO SEND ME ON A TWO-WEEK BUSINESS TRIP TO EUROPE.
EUROPE!!
WHAT'S WRONG WITH THAT?! LONDON! PARIS! ROME! MOM, MOM, CAN I COME? PLEASE??
I PROMISE I'LL BE GOOD. PLEASE? **PLEASE?? EUROPE!!**

I'D LIKE NOTHING BETTER, SWEETIE, BUT THE TRIP IS SCHEDULED DURING THE SCHOOL YEAR.
WAIT, WHAT? SCHOOL'S OVER NEXT WEEK.
NOT THIS SCHOOL YEAR.
THE TRIP IS SCHEDULED...
FOR SEPTEMBER.
SO THE THIRD SATURDAY IN SEPTEMBER...
I'M SUPPOSED TO BE IN VIENNA.

OKAY, SO...HAVE AN OCTOBER WEDDING! COOL AIR, THE LEAVES TURNING...
I DID THINK OF THAT, ACTUALLY.
I WAS SITTING AT MY DESK, MENTALLY ADDING SLEEVES TO OUR GOWNS AND CHANGING THE FLOWERS FROM ROSES TO CHRYSANTHEMUMS, WHEN THE PHONE RANG.
GUESS WHO IT WAS.
MOM, I'M NO GOOD AT GUESSING GAMES.
THE REAL ESTATE AGENT. SHE'S ALREADY FOUND A BUYER FOR OUR HOUSE.
WHAT?
THAT'S GREAT NEWS! YOU THOUGHT IT'D TAKE MONTHS, RIGHT?
WELL...
THE BUYER'S DESPERATE. HE'S WILLING TO PAY WHAT WE ASKED FOR, WHICH IS MORE THAN WE THOUGHT WE'D GET.
BUT THERE'S A CATCH: HE'S IN A RUSH.
HE WANTS TO MOVE HIS FAMILY IN BY JULY 15TH.

MOM, **NO!** THAT'S NEXT MONTH. IT'S IMPOSSIBLE. SELL THE HOUSE TO SOMEONE ELSE.
I DON'T THINK ANYONE ELSE WILL PAY US THIS MUCH MONEY.
WELL, WHAT DO WE NEED IT FOR? YOU'RE MARRYING **WATSON.**

SWEETIE, WATSON AND I AND WATSON'S EX-WIFE AND YOUR FATHER...
WE ALL HAVE VARIOUS IDEAS ABOUT HOW TO SPEND OUR MONEY.

IT'S COMPLICATED, BUT... LET'S JUST SAY THAT I DON'T WANT WATSON TO FEEL OBLIGED TO FINANCE FOUR EXTRA COLLEGE EDUCATIONS.

THE MONEY FROM THE HOUSE -- HALF OF WHICH IS YOUR FATHER'S -- IS GOING INTO A COLLEGE FUND FOR YOU AND YOUR BROTHERS.
SO THE MORE WE MAKE, THE BETTER.

AND THEN WITH WATSON'S PARENTS BEING AS RELIGIOUS AS THEY ARE, AND HIM NOT WANTING TO ROCK THE BOAT...
MOM, WHAT EXACTLY ARE YOU SAYING?

I'M SAYING THAT WATSON AND I ARE GOING TO HAVE TO GET MARRIED AT THE END OF THE MONTH... SO WE CAN MOVE INTO THE BREWERS' HOUSE TWO WEEKS LATER.

TWO AND A HALF WEEKS...TO PLAN A WEDDING.
UM...

TWO AND A HALF WEEKS!!

HOW CAN I PLAN A WHOLE WEDDING?! IT'S LIKE HAVING A **BABY**!
YOU NEED TIME TO **PREPARE** THINGS!
YOU HAVE TO TALK TO THE FLORIST, THE DRESSMAKER, THE CAKE SHOP...

KRISTY, WHAT'S GOING ON?
IT'S A LONG STORY.
AND THAT'S IF THE CATERER DOESN'T LAUGH AND HANG UP!!

WE'LL HAVE TO HAVE IT IN WATSON'S YARD. WE'D NEVER BE ABLE TO RENT A HALL FOR THE RECEPTION WITH SUCH SHORT NOTICE.
AND DECORATIONS!! WHAT IF IT RAINS?!
AND...
???
CLANG
mom!!!
CLUNK

MOM, WHAT ARE YOU DOING?!
WE HAVE TO GET READY TO **MOVE!**
THIS WHOLE HOUSE NEEDS TO BE PACKED UP! WE CAN... WE CAN CLEAN THINGS OUT. MAKE A BIG DONATION.
BUT --
I DON'T **WANNA** MOVE.
I WANT ONE MORE SUMMER HERE. I DON'T **WANNA** LEAVE YET.
I WANNA STAY **HEEEEERE.**
YOU SAID WE WEREN'T MOVING UNTIL THE FALL. YOU SAID I'D STILL HAVE THIS SUMMER...
WITH MY FRIENDS AND THE BABY-SITTERS CLUB AND...MY ROOM...
THOSE WEREN'T PROMISES, KRISTY.
I'M SORRY, BUT... THIS IS THE WAY THINGS HAVE TO BE.

WELL, I...
I JUST...
BOY.

A LOT OF THINGS HAVE HAPPENED HERE.
WHEN MARY ANNE'S STRICT DAD MADE HER GO TO BED EARLY, WE USED OUR SECRET FLASHLIGHT CODE TO KEEP TALKING LATE INTO THE NIGHT.
WHEN WE HAD FIGHTS, I KNEW I COULD ALWAYS GET TO HER BY PULLING MY WINDOW SHADE DOWN.
AND WHEN WE WEREN'T FIGHTING, WE COULD STRING A PAPER-CUP TELEPHONE OR SAIL PAPER PLANES BETWEEN OUR WINDOWS.
WHAT WAS I GOING TO DO WITHOUT MARY ANNE NEXT DOOR?
KRISTY?

SORRY, SWEETIE, BUT I REALLY NEED YOUR HELP DOWNSTAIRS.
ALL... ALL RIGHT.

IF WE'RE GOING TO PULL THIS OFF, WE'VE GOT TO START LISTING **EVERYTHING.** THINGS TO DO, THINGS TO BUY, PEOPLE TO CALL...

FIRST WE'LL DECIDE WHO TO INVITE. I'LL GO THROUGH OUR ADDRESS BOOK, AND YOU WRITE DOWN THE NAMES I CALL OUT.
GOT IT.

ALL OF US, OBVIOUSLY. NANNIE AND WATSON'S PARENTS.
BARB STARRS... THE BURGESSES...

...JIM AND RITA WILSON... AND I THINK THAT'S IT.
WHEW.

Hmm.
An awful lot of these people are from out of state, and a lot of them have children. They might not be able to take the time off, but we'll see.

And then we started in on other lists. Supplies we'd need to get, ideas for dinner, decorations...
Weddings sure are complicated.

By 5:30, when it was time for my Baby-sitters Club meeting, I understood why Mom was panicking earlier.

I began to feel sort of sorry for her.

WEDDING
SUMMER
TO DO
- cake tasting
- decorations!
- call florist
- invitations
- call caterers
TO INVITE
definitely:
- The Meners
- Watson's sister
- the Millers
- Mr. Brown
- the Spiers
- the Schafers

CHAPTER 3

BY THE TIME I DASHED ACROSS THE STREET TO CLAUDIA'S HOUSE, IT WAS 5:36 AND I WAS THE LAST ONE TO ARRIVE.
NOT A GREAT LOOK FOR THE CLUB PRESIDENT.
BUT SINCE EVERYONE WAS THERE ALREADY, I TOOK ADVANTAGE OF THE SITUATION TO GET A GOOD, LONG LOOK AT THEM.
STACEY MCGILL. CLUB TREASURER FROM NEW YORK, FASHION EXPERT.
MARY ANNE SPIER. CLUB SECRETARY, MY BEST FRIEND.

I KNEW I'D STILL SEE EVERYONE AT MEETINGS AND IN SCHOOL, BUT IT DIDN'T FEEL LIKE THINGS WOULD BE THE SAME AFTER I MOVED.
A-HA!
CLAUDIA KISHI. VICE PRESIDENT, ARTIST, CANDY AFICIONADA.
DAWN SCHAFER. ALTERNATE OFFICER, HEALTH NUT. HER MOM'S DATING MARY ANNE'S DAD.
MALLORY PIKE. JUNIOR OFFICER, OLDEST OF EIGHT -- SO SHE'S A REAL PRO.

SORRY I'M LATE.
ANY CALLS YET?
JUST ONE.

I HAVE A FEELING IT WAS SAM. HE WAS ASKING FOR A SITTER WHO HAD "EXPERIENCE WITH LOTS OF SMELLY FARTS."
THAT'S NOT EVEN **FUNNY.**

LET'S JUST MOVE ON TO CLUB BUSINESS.

LET'S SEE...HAVE YOU ALL BEEN READING THE NOTEBOOK?
YUP.
I'M CATCHING UP!

HOW'S THE TREASURY?
HEALTHY! WE'VE GOT A LITTLE EXTRA.

DO WE NEED ANYTHING?
I DON'T THINK SO. MAYBE WE SHOULD DO SOMETHING FUN.

OOH! AN END-OF-SCHOOL PARTY?

HOLD ON A MOMENT. KRISTY?
IS SOMETHING THE MATTER?
...
MIGHT AS WELL GET IT OVER WITH.
I...HAVE GOOD NEWS AND BAD NEWS.
UH-OH.
THE GOOD NEWS IS, I'M GOING TO BE A BRIDESMAID IN MOM'S WEDDING.
OOOOH.
THE BAD NEWS IS, THE WEDDING'S IN TWO AND A HALF WEEKS...
AND WE'RE MOVING IN JULY.

YOU CAN'T!
YOU CAN'T MOVE
IN JULY!!
I TRIED TO
TELL MOM THE
SAME THING.
SHE WOULDN'T LISTEN.
IT'S COMPLICATED, BUT
SHE HAS TO SELL THE
HOUSE RIGHT NOW.
BUT...
BUT...
ring
ring
HELLO,
BABY-SITTERS
CLUB.
HI, DR. JOHANSSEN!
HOW'S CHARLOTTE?
FRIDAY,
3 TO 5?
DAWN AND I
ARE FREE.
JEFF AND I ARE GOING
TO OUR GRANDPARENTS'
THAT AFTERNOON, SO
YOU CAN TAKE IT.

ALL RIGHT, KRISTY.
GOOD NEWS FIRST. TELL US ABOUT BEING A BRIDESMAID.
click
UH...
ACTUALLY, I'VE KNOWN SINCE SATURDAY, BUT I DIDN'T MENTION IT BECAUSE...
THEY WOULDN'T UNDERSTAND.
THEY'D HAVE SWAPPED THEIR OWN HOMES FOR WATSON'S IN AN INSTANT, GHOST AND ALL.
AND MARY ANNE WOULD HAVE BEEN OVERJOYED IF HER DAD HAD PROPOSED TO DAWN'S MOM.
HOW COULD I EXPLAIN THAT THE REASON I'D HARDLY TALKED ABOUT THE WEDDING WAS, DEEP DOWN...
I STILL WASN'T SURE I **WANTED** MOM AND WATSON TO GET MARRIED?
WELL, BECAUSE WE STILL THOUGHT THE WEDDING WAS MONTHS AND MONTHS AWAY.

OKAY, YOU GOOF, BUT TELL US ABOUT IT! WHAT ARE YOU GOING TO WEAR?
Poff

WELL...
ring
rin

CLAIRE AND MARGO, 3:30 TO 6 NEXT TUESDAY?
DAWN OR STACEY.
...

SORRY, I'M GOING TO BE AT THE DOCTOR IN NEW YORK ALL DAY.
EVERYTHING OKAY?
YEAH. JUST A CHECKUP.

BRIDESMAID GOWN.
OKAY, OKAY!

IT'S GOING TO BE LONG...

WITH SHORT SLEEVES...

POP!

AND A RIBBON SASH ABOVE MY WAIST. IT'LL MAKE ME LOOK TALLER.

POP!

AND YOUR SHOES?
OH! GET THIS!
MOM SAID I CAN WEAR HEELS, AND WE'RE GOING TO BUY THOSE SPECIAL SHOES THAT YOU CAN DYE TO MATCH YOUR DRESS.
OOOH!

AND ALL US KIDS ARE GOING TO BE IN THE WEDDING. EXCEPT ANDREW, HE'S SHY.
THAT'S SO CUTE!
I WISH I COULD BE IN A WEDDING.

AND YOU SAID IT WAS SOON, RIGHT?
A WEEK AFTER SCHOOL'S OUT.
WE'RE NEARLY FREEEEE!
flop

THAT REMINDS ME! ARE ANY OF YOU GOING TO THE FINAL FLING?

NOPE.
YOU DON'T NEED A DATE, YOU KNOW.
I DON'T LIKE DANCES.
WELL, I'M GOING. I JUST HAVE TO DECIDE WHAT TO WEAR.

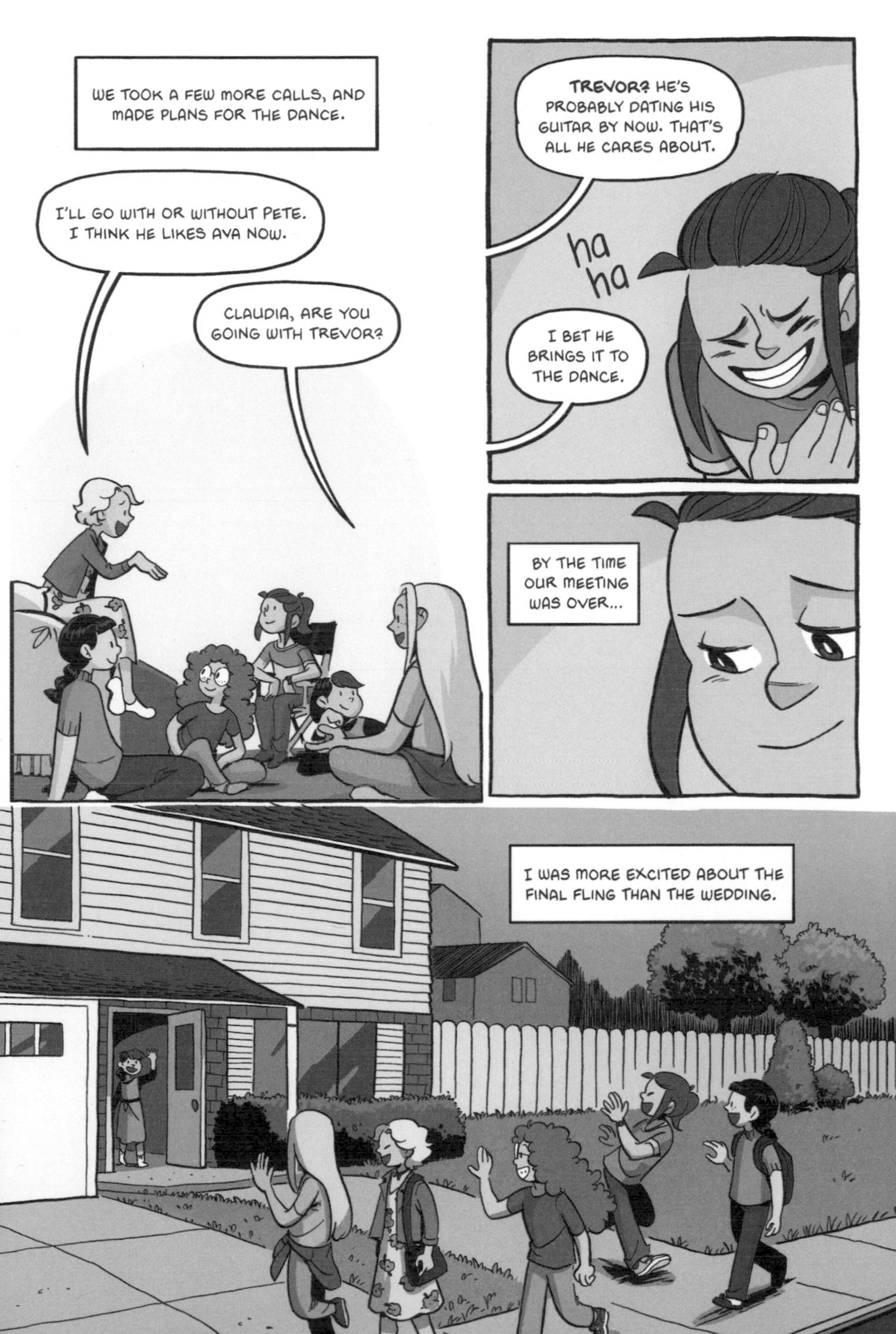
WE TOOK A FEW MORE CALLS, AND MADE PLANS FOR THE DANCE.
I'LL GO WITH OR WITHOUT PETE. I THINK HE LIKES AVA NOW.
CLAUDIA, ARE YOU GOING WITH TREVOR?
TREVOR? HE'S PROBABLY DATING HIS GUITAR BY NOW. THAT'S ALL HE CARES ABOUT.
ha ha
I BET HE BRINGS IT TO THE DANCE.
BY THE TIME OUR MEETING WAS OVER...
I WAS MORE EXCITED ABOUT THE FINAL FLING THAN THE WEDDING.

ADMIT ONE
Final FLING

CHAPTER 4

THE FINAL FLING CAME AND WENT.

I TOOK ALAN GRAY, LIKE USUAL.

HE WAS HIMSELF -- 50% PESTY, 50% FUN.

CLAUDIA BROUGHT AUSTIN BENTLEY, A NEW BOY IN SCHOOL, AND STACEY WENT WITH PETE AFTER ALL.

MR. SPIER AND MRS. SCHAFER INVITED DAWN AND MARY ANNE OUT FOR PIZZA, SO THEY SKIPPED.
AND THEN, BEFORE I KNEW IT, THE LAST DAY OF SCHOOL HAD COME AND GONE, TOO.
Pre-Algebra

IT WAS ONE WEEK AND ONE DAY BEFORE THE WEDDING.

MOM WAS TAKING THE FOLLOWING WEEK OFF FROM WORK TO GET EVERYTHING READY, AND TO MAKE UP FOR IT, SHE WAS WORKING EXTRA HARD AHEAD OF TIME.

OR SO I THOUGHT.

MOM! SHOULDN'T YOU BE AT WORK?!

THAT'S A TOUCHY QUESTION. I JUST ASKED HER THE SAME THING, AND YOU KNOW WHAT SHE SAID?

DON'T TELL ME, SAM. I'LL GUESS.

THE WEDDING'S IN FIVE DAYS AND WE'RE MOVING IN TWO WEEKS.
NO.

THE WEDDING'S TOMORROW AND WE'RE MOVING ON WEDNESDAY?
NO.

THE WEDDING'S IN FIVE MINUTES AND WE'RE MOVING TONIGHT?
NOOO.

BUT HOW ABOUT THIS?
WATSON'S EX-WIFE SUDDENLY HAD TO DROP OFF KAREN AND ANDREW.

AUNT COLLEEN AND UNCLE WALLACE ARE COMING EARLY TO HELP WITH WEDDING PREP AND ARE BRINGING THEIR KIDS.
AUNT THEO AND UNCLE NEAL, TOO.

AND --
UH-OH.

WATSON'S BEST FRIEND IS COMING SATURDAY EVENING. WITH HIS WIFE...AND THEIR FOUR CHILDREN.
MORE KIDS?
MM-HMM.
WHERE ARE ALL THESE PEOPLE GOING TO STAY?
OUR RELATIVES ARE STAYING AT THE HOLIDAY INN, AND WATSON'S FRIENDS ARE STAYING IN HIS SPARE ROOMS. BUT...
IF ALL THE ADULTS ARE HELPING OUT AT WATSON'S NEXT WEEK, THAT MEANS THERE'LL BE FOURTEEN CHILDREN RUNNING AROUND, TOO.
FOURTEEN?
ASHLEY, BERK, GRACE, PETER... EMMA, BETH, LUKE, ANDREW... KAREN AND DAVID MICHAEL... AND WATSON'S FRIEND'S KIDS?
KATHERINE, PATRICK, MAURA, AND TONY.
THAT'S... FOURTEEN, ALL RIGHT.
NEXT WEEK, I NEED ADULTS TO HELP ME COOK, ARRANGE FLOWERS, SET UP CHAIRS, SHOP, AND ABOUT A HUNDRED OTHER THINGS.
WE'RE NEVER GOING TO MANAGE ALL OF THAT WITH FOURTEEN CHILDREN UNDERFOOT.

HEY, MOM.
YES, KRISTY?
TODAY WAS THE LAST DAY OF SCHOOL.
OH HONEY, I'M SORRY. HOW WAS IT? DID YOU GET YOUR REPORT CARD?
STRAIGHT A'S, BUT THAT'S NOT WHAT I MEAN.

I MEAN THAT SCHOOL'S **OVER.** STARTING RIGHT NOW, I HAVE NOTHING TO DO -- EXCEPT BABY-SIT.

KRISTY, YOU'RE A GOOD, RESPONSIBLE BABY-SITTER, BUT EVEN YOU CAN'T TAKE CARE OF **FOURTEEN CHILDREN.**
NO...BUT THE BABY-SITTERS **CLUB** CAN.

THERE ARE SIX OF US. THE KIDS COULD COME OVER DURING THE DAY.
OH, BROTHER.

I'D HAVE TO CHECK WITH THE OTHER MEMBERS TO BE SURE, AND WE MIGHT HAVE TO CANCEL SOME APPOINTMENTS, BUT I THINK WE COULD DO IT.
KRISTY...THAT MIGHT BE THE SOLUTION!

IF WE COULD HIRE YOU FOR THE WEEK -- 9 TO 5, MONDAY THROUGH FRIDAY -- WATSON AND I WOULD PAY, LET'S SEE...
DOUBLE THE USUAL CLUB RATE.
WHAT!!
I VOLUNTEER! I'M OLD. I'M RESPONSIBLE. I LIVE WITH CHILDREN **EVERY DAY.**
SAM, YOU ALREADY **HAVE** A SUMMER JOB.
BOOOO.
KRISTY! KRISTY!
OH, MOM! YOU'RE HOME, TOO!
GUESS WHAT, EVERYBODY?

"CITIZENSHIP AWARD."
Citizenship Awa
"THIS CERTIFIES THAT DAVID MICHAEL THOMAS HAS BEEN CHOSEN BEST CITIZEN OF THE YEAR IN MR. BOWMAN'S ROOM, BY HIS PEERS."
Principal
Vice Principal
THAT MEANS THE OTHER KIDS. THEY **VOTED** FOR ME.
DUH.
HONEY, CONGRATULATIONS! WE'LL HAVE TO FRAME THIS.
CAN WE PUT IT ON THE AWARDS WALL?
OF **COURSE.**

YOU KNOW, IN ABOUT TWO WEEKS, THERE ISN'T GOING TO **BE** AN AWARDS WALL ANYMORE. WE'LL BE ALL PACKED UP FOR THE MOVE.
YEAH, I THOUGHT OF THAT. POOR KID.
DO YOU THINK MOM'LL PUT UP OUR AWARDS WALL AND TROPHY SHELF AT WATSON'S?
DUNNO.
HEY, SAM? WHAT DO YOU THINK ABOUT GOING TO THE BREWERS'?
I JUST FEEL LIKE IT'S GOING TO BE SO...
DIFFERENT.

WELL...I DON'T REALLY MIND. AT LEAST NONE OF US HAVE TO CHANGE SCHOOLS.
DID YOU KNOW THAT MOM AND WATSON HAVE TO PAY TO LET YOU STAY AT STONEYBROOK MIDDLE INSTEAD OF SWITCHING TO KELSEY?
WHAT? HOW COME?
WATSON IS IN KELSEY'S SCHOOL DISTRICT, SO YOU'RE SUPPOSED TO GO THERE. BUT THERE'S A SPECIAL FEE YOU CAN PAY TO IGNORE THAT.
Watson
Stonerbrook
Kelsey
CHARLIE AND I ARE GOOD, SINCE THERE'S ONLY ONE HIGH SCHOOL.
NOBODY TOLD ME.
THEY'RE TRYING TO MAKE THE MOVE AS EASY ON US AS POSSIBLE.
BUT...
SAM, WE STILL AREN'T WATSON'S KIDS. WE'LL BE LIVING OVER THERE, BUT WE'LL BE HIS STEPKIDS.
WHAT ARE YOU GETTING AT?
I DON'T KNOW WHAT THAT MEANS.
LIKE, IF WATSON WAS MY DAD, I COULD ASK HIM FOR BIG THINGS, LIKE A TV FOR MY BEDROOM. BUT HE'LL BE MY STEPDAD, SO WHAT'S THE LIMIT? CAN I BORROW A FEW DOLLARS WHEN MOM'S NOT AROUND? SHE WAS SAYING HE WON'T PAY FOR OUR COLLEGE.
THERE'S A BIG DIFFERENCE BETWEEN FOUR COLLEGE TUITIONS AND TWO DOLLARS.
YEAH, BUT...WHERE DO YOU DRAW THE LINE?
IN WHAT WAYS WILL HE BE OUR FATHER?
THOSE ARE HEAVY QUESTIONS.

SOUNDS LIKE YOU'VE BEEN HAVING ONE SERIOUS TALK.
I JUST WANT TO KNOW WHAT TO EXPECT, CHARLIE.
NO ONE KNOWS WHAT'S GOING TO HAPPEN, KRISTY. I DON'T THINK MOM AND WATSON ARE EVEN SURE.
UUUUUGH.
IT'S LIKE WE'RE IN A **MOVIE**. OUR PARENTS GET DIVORCED, MOM MEETS A **MILLIONAIRE**, THEY GET MARRIED, WE MOVE TO A MANSION.
BUT...
THAT DOESN'T MEAN IT HAS A HAPPY ENDING.
YEAH, I KNOW WHAT YOU MEAN. IT'S KIND OF NUTS.
AND SCARY. BUT WE'LL MAKE IT WORK.
YOU THINK SO?
YEAH.

CHAPTER 5

THE NEXT DAY, I CALLED THE FIRST EMERGENCY MEETING OF THE BABY-SITTERS CLUB THAT WE'D HAD IN A LONG TIME.
WHAT'S THIS ALL ABOUT?
YEAH, AN EMERGENCY ON THE FIRST DAY OF SUMMER VACATION?
WELL, SORT OF!
YOU ALL KNOW THAT THE WEDDING IS A WEEK AWAY. AND SINCE MOM HAS SO MUCH TO DO, MY RELATIVES AND SOME OF WATSON'S FRIENDS ARE COMING EARLY TO HELP.
THAT'S NICE.
IT IS, EXCEPT THAT THEY'RE ALL ARRIVING BY MONDAY -- WITH THEIR KIDS.
AT FIRST MOM THOUGHT THEY'D JUST HAVE TO HANG AROUND WATSON'S WHILE THE ADULTS WERE WORKING, BUT... I MADE A SUGGESTION.
IF WE BABY-SIT THE KIDS AT MY HOUSE, THE ADULTS CAN GET EVERYTHING DONE.
THE ONLY THING IS...
THERE ARE FOURTEEN OF THEM.
FOURTEEN?
BUT WE'VE BABY-SAT FOR LOTS OF KIDS BEFORE.
I KNOW WE CAN DO THIS. AND MOM SAID THAT IF WE CAN WATCH THEM FROM 9 TO 5 EVERY DAY, SHE AND WATSON WILL PAY EACH OF US...

TWICE OUR USUAL RATE.

THAT'S A LOT OF GUMMY BEARS.

hahahah
OR THREE HUNDRED TWINKIES!
LIKE SIXTY BAGS!
TWELVE HUNDRED JAWBREAKERS!

YOU'RE SERIOUS ABOUT THIS, RIGHT?
OF COURSE I'M SERIOUS.

MOM'S IN A REAL BIND. WE DIDN'T SEE THIS COMING.
AND WITH EVERYONE COMING FROM OUT OF TOWN... WE HAVE TO DO SOMETHING.

AND YOUR MOM THINKS WE CAN HANDLE IT?
YES. SO DO I. IT WORKS OUT TO TWO OR THREE KIDS FOR EACH OF US.
THAT'S NOTHING.

BUT FOURTEEN KIDS AT **ONCE.**
A MILLION BALLS OF REALLY NICE YARN.

WHAT DO YOU GUYS THINK?

I'M IN.
LET'S DO THIS.

WE CAN DO IT.
YEAH!

MARY ANNE?

...LET'S DO IT.
ALL RIGHT!
THAT MEANS WE HAVE SOME SERIOUS PLANNING TO DO. 9 TO 5 MEANS ALL DAY, EVERY DAY NEXT WEEK.
I'M GOING TO HAVE TO LEAVE A COUPLE OF TIMES FOR DRESS FITTINGS AND THINGS, BUT IT SHOULDN'T BE TOO MUCH. MARY ANNE, CAN YOU CHECK NEXT WEEK'S CALENDAR?
LET'S SEE...
THIS ISN'T TOO BAD.
KRISTY, YOU'RE SCHEDULED FOR JAMIE NEWTON ON TUESDAY. I'VE GOT JENNY PREZZIOSO WEDNESDAY EVENING, AND I CAN STILL DO THAT...
THEN, STACEY, YOU'RE SITTING FOR CHARLOTTE JOHANSSEN ON THURSDAY. THE ONLY OTHER APPOINTMENTS ARE DAVID MICHAEL, KAREN, AND ANDREW, BUT WE'LL HAVE THEM ANYWAY.
2
3
4
5
Stacey—
Charlotte J.
Mary Anne—
Jenny P.
HMM.
WE'LL HAVE TO CALL THE NEWTONS AND JOHANSSENS AND CANCEL. UNLESS...
WE COULD JUST BRING THEM OVER!
I'LL CALL MRS. NEWTON, THEN YOU CALL DR. JOHANSSEN.

I EXPLAINED THE SITUATION TO MRS. NEWTON, WHO WAS NOT ONLY UNDERSTANDING, BUT ENTHUSIASTIC.
SHE THOUGHT THE EXPERIENCE WOULD BE GOOD FOR JAMIE, WHO WAS GOING TO PRESCHOOL IN THE FALL AND NEEDED TO GET USED TO HAVING OTHER KIDS AROUND.

AND AS IT TURNED OUT, DR. JOHANSSEN WAS JUST ABOUT TO CALL **US** -- HER SCHEDULE HAD GOTTEN SWITCHED AROUND, SO SHE DIDN'T NEED A SITTER AFTER ALL.

ALL RIGHT, I'D BETTER TELL YOU ABOUT THE KIDS.
I'LL TAKE NOTES.

FIRST, THERE ARE THE MILLERS.
(cousins)
Ashley (9)
Berk (6)
Grace (5)
Peter (3)

THEN THE MEINERS. I HAVEN'T MET BETH YET, BUT HER PICTURES ARE CUTE.
(cousins)
Emma (8)
Luke (10)
Beth (1)

AND LAST, THE FIELDINGS. I DON'T KNOW A LOT ABOUT THEM.
(Watson's friends)
GOSH.
Patrick (3)
Katherine (5)
Maura (2)
Tony (8mo.)

WELL, I COUNT A TEN-YEAR-OLD, TWO SIX-YEAR-OLDS, ONE NINE-YEAR-OLD, ONE EIGHT-YEAR-OLD, A FOUR-YEAR-OLD, ONE SEVEN-YEAR-OLD, TWO FIVE-YEAR-OLDS, TWO THREE-YEAR-OLDS, A ONE-YEAR-OLD, A TWO-YEAR-OLD...
AND A BABY.
IT SOUNDS LIKE KIND OF A HANDFUL WHEN YOU PUT IT THAT WAY.
BUT WE'LL MANAGE. MAYBE WE SHOULD ORGANIZE THE LIST? SORT THE KIDS BY AGE AND DIVIDE THEM UP.
ON IT.
scribble
Luke - 10
Ashley - 9
Emma - 8
David M. - 7
Berk - 6
Karen - 6
Grace - 5
Katherine - 5
Andrew - 4
Peter - 3
Patrick - 3
Maura - 2
Beth - 1
Tony - 8mo.
OOOOH.

LET ME SEE THAT.

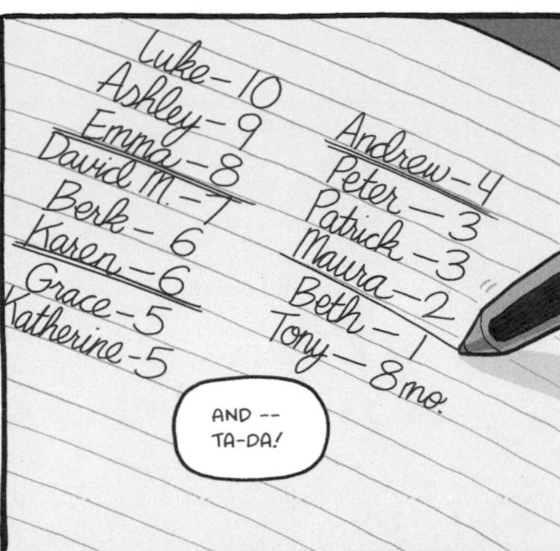
Luke–10
Ashley–9
Emma–8
David M.–7
Berk–6
Karen–6
Grace–5
Katherine–5
Andrew–4
Peter–3
Patrick–3
Maura–2
Beth–1
Tony–8 mo.
AND -- TA-DA!

NOW WE HAVE FIVE GROUPS OF KIDS -- MALLORY CAN BE WITH ME, SINCE I'LL BE HOPPING OUT FOR WEDDING STUFF SOMETIMES.
WE'D BETTER DECIDE WHO'LL BE IN CHARGE OF EACH GROUP.

DOES ANYONE ESPECIALLY WANT THE OLDER KIDS?

THE BABIES?

I DON'T REALLY CARE WHICH KIDS I GET.
SAME.

DAWN GOT THE SIX- AND SEVEN-YEAR-OLDS, THE TWO- AND THREE-YEAR-OLDS WENT TO CLAUDIA, AND MALLORY AND I TOOK GRACE, KATHERINE, AND ANDREW.

THAT MAKES SENSE, SINCE ANDREW'S MOST COMFORTABLE AROUND ME.
AND JAMIE'S ABOUT THE SAME AGE, SO WE CAN TAKE HIM ON TUESDAY.

HEY! YOU KNOW WHAT WE CAN DO TO KEEP THE GROUPS STRAIGHT?

WE COULD CALL THEM THE RED GROUP OR BLUE GROUP OR WHATEVER, AND MAKE RED NAME TAGS FOR STACEY'S KIDS, BLUE FOR DAWN'S, AND SO ON.
THAT WAY WE CAN LEARN EVERYONE'S NAMES AND SPOT OUR KIDS QUICKLY, TOO.
YES!!

WE'LL NEED CONSTRUCTION PAPER, STRING...

OH, AND WE SHOULD MAKE MATCHING TAGS FOR OURSELVES.
THAT WAY, ALL THE KIDS WILL BE ABLE TO FIND THEIR LEADER, EVEN THE ONES WHO CAN'T READ YET.
THAT'S A GOOD IDEA.

WHEW!
Luke
Grace
Ashley
Emma
Andy
HELLO, GIRLS.
YOU SEEM TO BE WORKING VERY HARD.
CLAUDIA FILLED MIMI IN ON WHAT WE WERE DOING.
OH MY!
YOU **MUST** BE SURE TO CALL ON ME IF YOU NEED ANYTHING. I WILL BE HAPPY TO HELP OUT.
THANK YOU, MIMI. THAT'S REALLY GOOD TO KNOW.
WE WERE ALL STILL A LITTLE NERVOUS...
BUT WE STARTED TO GET EXCITED AS WE TALKED, PLANNED, AND MADE LISTS OF THINGS TO DO WITH THE KIDS.
MONDAY COULDN'T COME SOON ENOUGH!

Beth
Stacey
Red Star Group
•Luke (10)
•Ashley (9)
•Emma (8)
Dawn
Bluebird Group
•David Michael (7)
•Berk (6)
•Karen (6)
Kristy & Mallory
Yellow Sun Group
•Grace (5)
•Katherine (5)
•Andrew (4)
Claudia
Green Dinosaur Group
•Peter (3)
•Patrick (3)
•Maura (2)
Mary Anne
Pink Heart Group
•Beth (1)
•Tony (8 mo.)

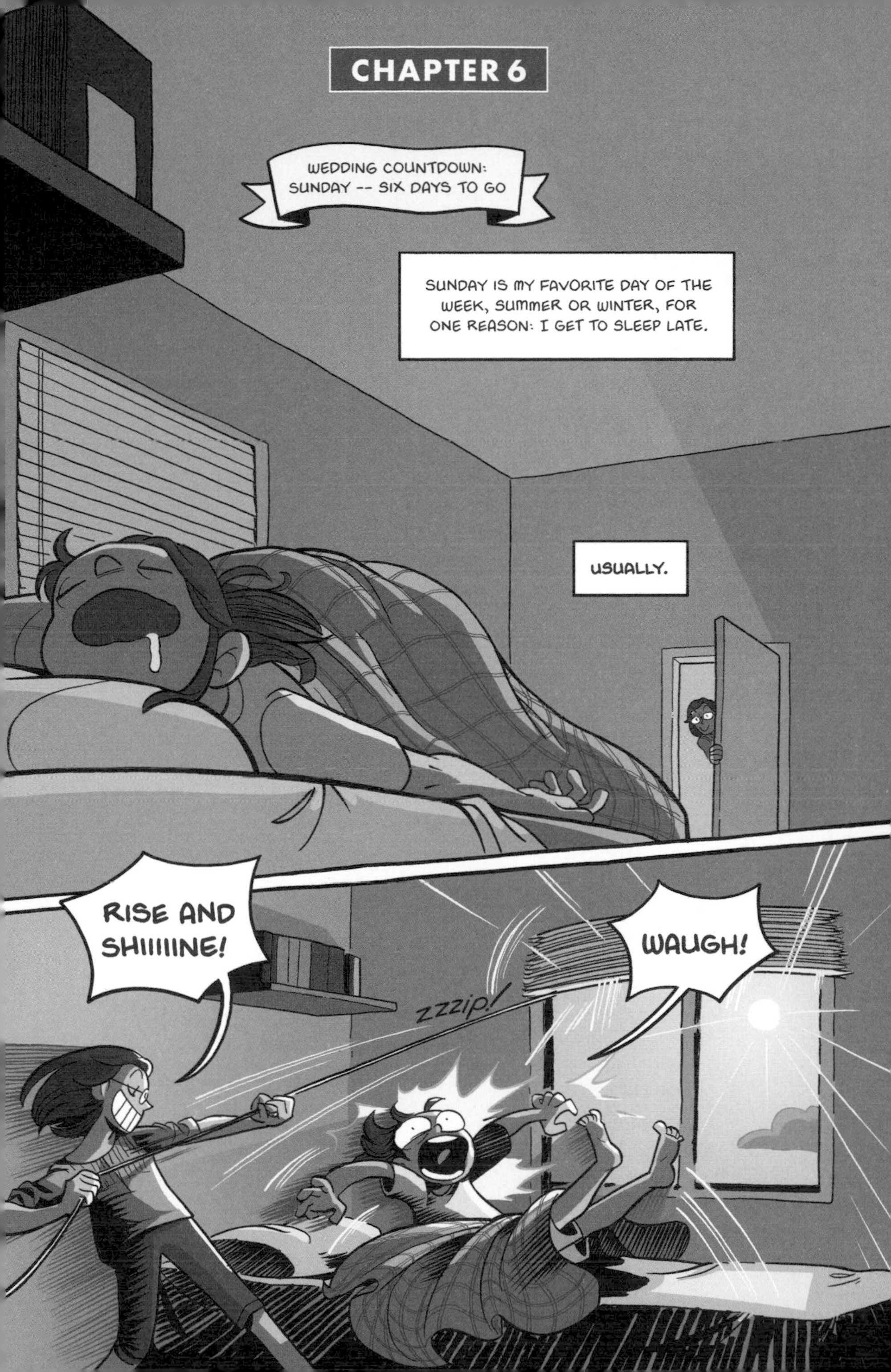
CHAPTER 6
WEDDING COUNTDOWN: SUNDAY -- SIX DAYS TO GO
SUNDAY IS MY FAVORITE DAY OF THE WEEK, SUMMER OR WINTER, FOR ONE REASON: I GET TO SLEEP LATE.
USUALLY.
RISE AND SHIIIIINE!
zzzip!
WAUGH!

WHY ARE YOU TORTURING ME?!
IT'S EIGHT O'CLOCK! EVEN YOUR BROTHERS ARE UP ALREADY.
fling!

BUT I WON'T HAVE ANOTHER CHANCE TO SLEEP IN UNTIL NEXT SUNDAAAAAY!
KRISTY!

I NEED YOU TODAY.
UUUUUUGH.

AUNT COLLEEN, UNCLE WALLACE, AUNT THEO, AND UNCLE NEAL ARE ARRIVING TODAY.
THEY'RE GOING TO THE MOTEL FIRST, AND THEN THEY'LL COME HERE FOR DINNER.

AND NANNIE'S COMING OVER. SHE WANTS TO MEASURE YOU AGAIN.
MMPH.

ARE YOU SURE I CAN'T SLEEP FOR JUST TEN MORE MINUTES?
OUT WE GO!

A FEW HOURS LATER, I WENT OUTSIDE TO WAIT FOR NANNIE.
NANNIE IS MY GRANDMA ON MOM'S SIDE. SHE LIVES ABOUT FORTY MINUTES AWAY, AND SHE'S REALLY COOL. SHE DOES A BUNCH OF STUFF, LIKE GARDENING AND BOWLING -- AND SEWING.
SHE EVEN VOLUNTEERED TO MAKE DRESSES FOR ME AND KAREN!

HONK!

NANNIE!
HELLOOOOO!
honk! honk!

NANNIE! HOW'S MY DRESS?
KRISTYYYY. AT LEAST WAIT UNTIL SHE'S INSIDE.
OH, SHE'S JUST EXCITED.

IT'S COMING ALONG WONDERFULLY. I JUST NEED TO CHECK THE ARMS AGAIN.

IT'LL BE READY IN TIME, RIGHT? RIGHT??
KRISTY!

WE ALL TOOK A FEW MINUTES TO DRINK LEMONADE AND CATCH UP WITH NANNIE...

AND THEN IT WAS TIME FOR BUSINESS.

WHILE US KIDS CLEANED THE HOUSE...

MOM AND NANNIE HOLED UP IN THE KITCHEN TO FIGURE OUT WEDDING FOOD.

MOM HAD BEEN LUCKY ENOUGH TO FIND A CATERER WHO COULD MAKE THE MAIN COURSE ON SHORT NOTICE, BUT SHE AND WATSON WERE ON THEIR OWN FOR EVERYTHING ELSE.

THEY'D HAVE TO SHOW THE OTHER ADULTS HOW TO PREPARE **HUNDREDS** OF APPETIZERS, SALADS, AND DESSERTS.

BY LATE AFTERNOON, THE HOUSE WAS SHINY AND CLEAN...
MOM AND NANNIE WERE THROUGH WITH RECIPES FOR THE TIME BEING...
AND OUR RELATIVES WERE STARTING TO ARRIVE.
HONK!
THEY'RE HERE! THEY'RE HERE!!
HONK!

UNCLE NEAL. HE ALWAYS SMELLS LIKE CIGARS, BUT HE'S OKAY.
AUNT THEO, MOM'S YOUNGER SISTER.
KRISTY, HOW YOU'VE GROWN!
hug!
SHE SAYS THAT TO EVERYONE, AND I MOST CERTAINLY HAVE NOT.
EMMA, WHO'S ALWAYS A BUNDLE OF ENERGY...
NANNIE! NANNIE! I WON A SECOND-PLACE RIBBON IN MY GYMNASTICS MEET!
AND LUKE, WHO I REMEMBERED AS BEING SMALL AND KIND OF QUIET.
LOOKS LIKE THE LAST TWO YEARS HAVEN'T CHANGED HIM MUCH.
AND...
HI THERE, BETH.

slide

BOOP.
tickle!

hee hee

GOODNESS!

I'M AMAZED SHE LET YOU PICK HER UP! USUALLY, SHE SCREAMS IF STRANGERS GET ANYWHERE CLOSE.

WE HAVE THE **WORST** TIME WITH BABY-SITTERS.

BEEP BEEP!

AUNT COLLEEN!
UNCLE WALLACE!

HEY, KRISTY!
COLLEEN IS MY MOM'S YOUNGEST SISTER, AND I LOVE HER.

SHE'S A LOT LIKE NANNIE -- BUSY AND ACTIVE, WITH A BIT OF A WILD STREAK.
HOW YOU DOING, HON?
FINE.

MEANWHILE, COUSINS WERE SPILLING OUT OF THE CAR.
BERK!!

PETER? YOU OKAY?
HE'S A LITTLE CARSICK.

YEAH, HE JUST PUKED ALL OVER HIS ACTIVITY BOOK!
GRACE, THAT'S ENOUGH.

ASHLEY! WHAT HAPPENED TO YOU?
I BROKE IT ROLLER-SKATING.

WE DIDN'T MENTION IT BECAUSE WE DIDN'T WANT ANYONE TO THINK WE SHOULDN'T COME.
SHE'S ACTUALLY PRETTY FAST.

HE WASN'T KIDDING!

NANNIE FUSSED OVER ASHLEY, AND THEN HANDED OUT GIFTS TO ALL THE KIDS.

EVEN MY BROTHERS AND ME, ALTHOUGH WE SEE HER PRETTY OFTEN!

THEN IT WAS TIME FOR DINNER, AND OH **BOY.**

BETH SPIT A HUGE MOUTHFUL OF CARROTS ALL OVER HER DAD'S SHIRT.
spit

PETER AND GRACE GOT INTO A FIGHT AND BEGAN TO CRY.

BERK AND DAVID MICHAEL GOT INTO A FIGHT AND BEGAN TO CRY.

EMMA TEASED ASHLEY. ASHLEY WHACKED EMMA WITH HER CRUTCH. EMMA CRIED.
THEY WERE SENT TO SEPARATE ROOMS UNTIL THEY APOLOGIZED.

AND LUKE DID NOT SAY ONE WORD FOR THE ENTIRE MEAL.

THESE EIGHT KIDS WERE CAUSING PLENTY OF TROUBLE, EVEN WITH SEVEN ADULTS, ME, SAM, AND CHARLIE THERE.

gulp
WHAT WOULD THE NEXT DAY BE LIKE -- WITH JUST **SIX** BABY-SITTERS WATCHING **FOURTEEN** CHILDREN?

CHAPTER 7

WEDDING COUNTDOWN: MONDAY -- 5 DAYS TO GO
IT'S ONLY FOURTEEN KIDS.

THEY'RE ALL SHORTER THAN YOU.
ding dong

8:30 ON THE DOT!
I ALMOST COULDN'T SLEEP.

LET'S PUT ON OUR OWN TAGS BEFORE WE FORGET THEM.
THEN WE BETTER GET ORGANIZED.

IT'S GORGEOUS OUT. MAYBE WE SHOULD TRY TO STAY IN THE BACKYARD.
YEAH. IF THINGS GET CRAZY, WE CAN ALWAYS BREAK INTO GROUPS.

AND, MARY ANNE, MOM GOT OUT OUR OLD PLAYPEN IN CASE YOU NEED IT.
THAT'S PERFECT! I'LL SET IT UP OUTSIDE SO TONY AND BETH CAN BE WITH THE BIG KIDS.

JUST BEFORE NINE O'CLOCK, THE MILLERS ARRIVED.

NOW, WE'VE SPLIT YOU UP INTO DIFFERENT GROUPS.
Berk
Grace

YOUR TAGS LOOK LIKE YOUR LEADER'S, SO YOU CAN SPOT EACH OTHER.
KRISTY!

I KNOW YOU AND YOUR FRIENDS WILL HAVE YOUR HANDS FULL TODAY, BUT I NEED TO TELL YOU A COUPLE OF THINGS.

PETER USUALLY GOES DOWN FOR A NAP AFTER LUNCH -- AROUND TWO. GRACE GENERALLY DOESN'T TAKE A NAP, BUT IF SHE'S CRANKY, SHE'LL SOMETIMES GO
PETER. BERK HAS
UM... JUST ONE SECOND.

?

??

PLEASE, CONTINUE.

THESE ARE PRESCRIPTIONS.
MAKE SURE THEY'RE OUT OF REACH OF THE SMALL CHILDREN. YOU SHOULDN'T NEED THEM, BUT YOU MIGHT.
THE ONE WITH THE PINK CAP IS FOR BERK'S ALLERGIES. IF YOU'RE OUTDOORS A LOT AND HE STARTS WHEEZING, GIVE HIM ONE OF THESE AND MAKE SURE HE LIES DOWN INSIDE FOR A WHILE. HE'LL KNOW WHAT TO DO.
OH BOY.
WHAT IF ONE OF THE KIDS GOT SICK AND WE HAD TO SPLIT THEM OFF FROM THE GROUP?
AND THE OTHER ONE IS FOR ASHLEY.
WAS OUR HOUSE CHILDPROOF ENOUGH? HAD WE REALLY THOUGHT EVERYTHING THROUGH?
IF HER LEG STARTS SWELLING OR HURTING, YOU CAN GIVE HER HALF A PILL WITH FOOD.
GOT IT.
I THINK THAT'S IT.
THANK YOU, KRISTY.
YOO-HOO! KRISTY! WE'RE HEE-EEEERE!

AUNT THEO, THIS IS MARY ANNE, STACEY --

FINE, FINE, YES. THANK YOU.

NOW, I'VE BROUGHT BETH'S WALK-A-TOT CHAIR SO SHE CAN SCOOT AROUND SAFELY, AND HER STROLLER IF YOU WANT TO TAKE A WALK. IT MIGHT ALSO HELP IF SHE CRIES -- SHE'LL PROBABLY DO THAT WHEN WE LEAVE.

BETH USUALLY TAKES TWO NAPS, AROUND ELEVEN AND TWO, AND SHE TENDS TO TAKE A BOTTLE TO BED WITH HER.

SHE'S ALLERGIC TO COW'S MILK, SO MAKE SURE YOU **ONLY** GIVE HER THE BOTTLES I BROUGHT.

I'M GONNA DRAW
MORBIDDA DESTINY!

HONEY, I WANT YOU TO MEET MR. AND MRS. FIELDING.
HI.

I'M KRISTY. AND THESE ARE THE OTHER MEMBERS OF THE BABY-SITTERS CLUB.

THEY'RE ALL VERY SHY.
DUH.

THIS IS WHERE YOU'RE GOING TO PLAY TODAY. ANDREW AND KAREN ARE HERE. SEE?

I'M KRISTY. WE'RE GOING TO HAVE LOTS OF FUN.

THERE ARE GAMES AND TOYS AND FRIENDS TO PLAY WITH.

UM, DO YOU LIKE DOGS? WE'VE GOT OLD LOUIE –
A DOG??

...
I THINK I'M JUST GOING TO PUT TONY IN THE PLAYPEN, IF THAT'S ALL RIGHT.

WAHHHH HHHHHH HHHHHH

WAHHHHHHHHHHHHHHAHHHH
I, UM, HE'LL STOP CRYING. AFTER A WHILE.
THIS IS KATHERINE.
AND THESE ARE PATRICK AND MAURA.

WELL! ARE THE ADULTS ALL READY TO GO?
YES! LET'S.

WAHHHH

QUICK! PUT ON THE REST OF THE NAME TAGS AND DIVIDE INTO GROUPS.
GO! GO! GO!
WAHHHWAHHHH!
grab!
AND JUST LIKE THAT, OUR FIRST CRISIS WAS AVERTED.

THEN NANNIE WHISKED KAREN AND ME AWAY TO LOOK AT WEDDING FLOWERS.

WE SPENT FIFTEEN MINUTES DISCUSSING FLOWER COLORS...

AND THEN FORTY MINUTES DECIDING HOW WE WOULD DO OUR HAIR.

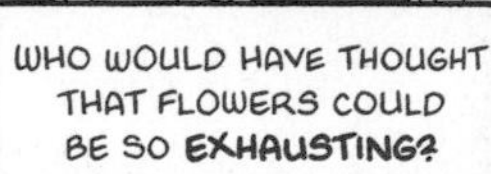

I DIDN'T KNOW WHETHER I'D HAVE THE ENERGY TO DEAL WITH WHAT I FOUND WHEN WE GOT HOME, BUT AS IT TURNED OUT...

COMING BACK WAS THE NICEST PART OF THE DAY.

THE LITTLE KIDS WERE RESTED FROM THEIR NAPS AND STORIES.

AND THE OLDER KIDS WERE EXCITED BECAUSE STACEY AND DAWN HAD HELPED THEM PUT TOGETHER A PLAY --
WHICH THEY PERFORMED FOR ALL OF US!

AT FIVE O'CLOCK, THE PARENTS CAME HOME TO FOURTEEN HAPPY CHILDREN.

OUR FIRST DAY, TO EVERYONE'S SURPRISE...

HAD BEEN A SUCCESS.

TUESDAY, JUNE 23

TODAY WAS ANOTHER BRIGHT, SUNNY DAY, THANK GOODNESS, AND ALMOST AS WARM AS A NICE SEPTEMBER DAY IN CALIFORNIA. YESTERDAY WAS FINE WITH ALL THE KIDS IN KRISTY'S BACKYARD, BUT WE DECIDED TO DO DIFFERENT THINGS THIS MORNING. THE KIDS WOULD GET TIRED OF THE THOMASES' YARD PRETTY QUICKLY. SO AFTER THE PARENTS LEFT, MARY ANNE TOOK THE BABIES FOR A WALK, STACEY TOOK THE RED GROUP TO THE BROOK TO CATCH MINNOWS, KRISTY AND CLAUDIA WALKED THEIR GROUPS TO THE PUBLIC LIBRARY FOR STORY HOUR, AND I TOOK DAVID MICHAEL, BERK, AND KAREN TO THE SCHOOL PLAYGROUND.

WHAT A MORNING MY GROUP HAD - ALL THANKS TO KAREN'S IMAGINATION.

- DAWN

CHAPTER 8

WEDDING COUNTDOWN:
TUESDAY -- 4 DAYS TO GO

TUESDAY STARTED OFF A LOT LIKE MONDAY, BUT WITH LESS CRYING ON THE KIDS' PARTS AND MORE CONFIDENCE ON OURS.

TODAY, WE'D BE SPLITTING UP FOR GROUP ACTIVITIES.

MARY ANNE WAS HAVING A PEACEFUL, IF SLOW, GO OF IT.

BETH AND TONY BOTH STARTED IN THE STROLLER, BUT THEN BETH WANTED TO GET OUT AND WALK.

SHE WASN'T VERY GOOD AT WALKING YET.

AFTER TEN MINUTES, THEY'D TRAVELED ABOUT SIX FEET.

MEANWHILE, STACEY SET OFF FOR THE BROOK WITH LUKE, ASHLEY, AND EMMA.
I CAN'T GET INTO A GOOD POSITION! MY LEG JUST WON'T GO THAT WAY.
OH NO, YOU'RE RIGHT. UM...
I HAVE A BETTER IDEA.
WHAT'S A PIRATE'S FAVORITE LETTER?
ARRRRRR!
NO, THE SEA!!
BOOOOOOO.

CLAUDIA, MALLORY, AND I HAD BUNDLED OUR KIDS INTO A FEW WAGONS, SO WE WERE MAKING GOOD TIME ON OUR WAY TO THE LIBRARY.
LEGS **IN** THE WAGON!

THE ONLY HITCH CAME WHEN WE STOPPED TO PICK UP JAMIE.
HI-HI!

Hmmmm.

HEY, YOU KNOW WHAT WE NEED? A **WAGON WATCHER.**

YELL IF YOU SEE ANYONE PUT THEIR HANDS OR FEET OUTSIDE THE WAGON. THEN YOU HAVE TO TRADE PLACES.

CLAUDIA'S IDEA WAS GREAT.
NONE OF THE KIDS WANTED TO BE CAUGHT, BUT THEY ALL WANTED TO **BE** THE WAGON WATCHER.
hee hee hee hee

SO WE ROLLED CHEERFULLY TO THE LIBRARY, STOPPING EIGHT TIMES TO SWITCH KIDS, AND ARRIVED JUST IN TIME FOR STORY HOUR.

WHILE ALL OF THIS WAS HAPPENING, DAWN WAS WALKING THE BLUEBIRDS TO THE ELEMENTARY SCHOOL PLAYGROUND FOR AN ARTS-AND-CRAFTS GROUP.
BUT MORBIDDA DIDN'T KNOW I HAD ONE MORE SPELL LEFT TO SAAAAAAY!
IT SOUNDED LIKE AN EASY JOB, AND THAT'S HOW IT STARTED OUT...
AND THE GOOD MAAAAGIC BLEW HER UP, UP, AND AWAYYYY!
BUT KAREN BREWER ALWAYS SEEMS TO MAKE THINGS MORE INTERESTING THAN USUAL.
HEY, DAVID MICHAEL, YOU KNOW WHAT?
WHAT?
YESTERDAY WHEN I GOT HOME, THIS BIG KID ON MY STREET SAID...
THAT AN ARMY OF **MARTIANS** IS GOING TO ATTACK TONIGHT.
MARTIANS?!
TONIGHT?!
KAREN, YOU KNOW THAT'S JUST A STORY. A JOKE.
IT'S **TRUE!** HE TOLD ME A LOT OF PEOPLE WOULD THINK THAT, BUT THE **BELIEVERS** WOULD BE ABLE TO HIDE IN TIME.
SO IF WE MAKE IT UNDERGROUND BEFORE THEY ATTACK, WE'LL BE SAFE.

YOU GUYS --
I WONDER WHAT'LL HAPPEN WHEN THEY LAND.
I BET THEY HAVE RAY GUNS! AND **SPRAY** GUNS!

AND THERE'LL BE **HUNDREDS** OF THEM COMING, IN BIG SHINY SILVER SAUCERS.
AUUUUUUGH!

I THOUGHT I **SAW** ONE!
thud

GUYS, WE'RE **HERE**! THEY'VE GOT ARTS AND CRAFTS TODAY.
AND A PUPPET-MAKING CONTEST!
Arts + Crafts Inside!

WOULDN'T YOU LIKE TO ENTER? I WONDER WHAT THE PRIZE --
KAREN? YOUR BASEMENT IS UNDERGROUND, RIGHT? CAN WE HIDE THERE?
I DON'T KNOW IF OUR MOTEL HAS A BASEMENT.

Arts + Crafts Inside!

COME ON, YOU GUYS.
WHY DON'T WE TRY
MAKING SOME PUPPETS?

WE'D RATHER
GO SWING.
OOOKAY. I'LL GO
SEE WHAT THAT
PRIZE IS, AT LEAST.

FRAN!
FRAAAAAN!

TINA! WHAT'S WRONG?

MARTIANS!! THEY'RE COMING TO TAKE US AWAY!
WHAT ON EARTH?

...WHICH MEANS YOU'LL HAVE TO GO UNDERGROUND.
LIKE IN YOUR BASEMENT.

KAREN BREWER.
I'M GOING HOME!!
ME TOOOOOO!!

I DO NOT WANT YOU SCARING THE OTHER KIDS WITH THAT STORY.
BUT WE HAVE TO WARN THEM. THEY HAVE TO BE READY FOR THE ATTACK!
THERE'S NO SUCH THING.

NOW LET'S GO MAKE SOME PUPPETS.

crack!
CRASH!
MARTIANS!
AHHHHHH!

THEY'RE COMING TO GET US! THEY'RE ATTACKING! WE HAVE TO HIDE! HURRY, HURRY!!
AHHHHHH

I AM SO, SO SORRY.
JUST... GET HER OUT OF HERE, ALL RIGHT?

KAREN...
WHAT YOU DID WAS VERY BAD.

YOU SCARED A LOT OF KIDS TODAY. NOW THINK ABOUT WHAT'S GOING TO HAPPEN TONIGHT, WHEN THEY GO HOME AND CAN'T GET TO SLEEP.

WHAT IF ONE OF THEM DOES SOMETHING DANGEROUS AND GETS HURT, BECAUSE OF THE SCARY STORIES YOU TOLD?
...I'M SORRY.

I PROMISE TO NEVER MENTION THE MARTIANS AGAIN.
ME TOO.
YEAH.

YOU'RE A VERY GOOD STORYTELLER, KAREN.
I KNOW.
David Michael

THE REST OF TUESDAY PASSED CALMLY, AND WE WENT OUR SEPARATE WAYS -- EXHAUSTED, BUT PROUD OF OURSELVES FOR MAKING IT THROUGH ANOTHER DAY.
I SHOULD HAVE BEEN PATTING MYSELF ON THE BACK AS I DRIFTED PEACEFULLY TO SLEEP.
BUT SOMETHING HAD JUST OCCURRED TO ME.
click
WAS I SUPPOSED TO GET MOM AND WATSON A WEDDING PRESENT?

Wednesday, June 24

This is a confession, you guys. I know you think I'm so sophisticated, since I'm from New York and everything, but no kidding, my favorite movie is "Mary Poppins." I've seen it 65 times. I know it by heart. Anyway, when I saw that it was going to be at the Embassy Theater for a special screening, I decided I had to have another chance to see it on a big screen. That's one reason I was so determined to take the red group to it. Besides, since it's my favorite movie, I was sure Luke, Emma, and Ashley would love it, too. Believe me, if I'd had a crystal ball to see into the future, I would never have taken them.

Stacey

CHAPTER 9

WEDDING COUNTDOWN:
WEDNESDAY -- THREE DAYS TO GO

1:00 ON WEDNESDAY MARKED OUR OFFICIAL HALFWAY POINT. JUST TWO AND A HALF DAYS LEFT!

WE HAVE THREE BATHROOMS: ONE DOWNSTAIRS AND TWO UPSTAIRS. MOM'S IS UPSTAIRS AND OFF-LIMITS, WHICH MEANT WE HAD TO SHARE TWO BATHROOMS BETWEEN TWENTY PEOPLE.

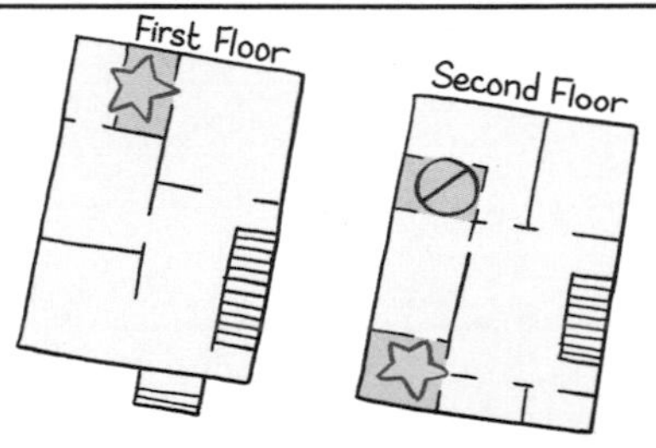

THE MOST IMPORTANT THING WAS THAT THE KIDS WERE HAVING FUN. AND STACEY HAD A VERY SPECIAL PLAN FOR HER GROUP THAT AFTERNOON.

WHILE NANNIE AND I WENT SHOE SHOPPING, STACEY WOULD BE TAKING HER KIDS TO SEE MARY POPPINS.

TRUE TO HER POSITION AS TREASURER, SHE'D EVEN THOUGHT AHEAD AND ASKED THEIR PARENTS FOR PERMISSION AND TICKET MONEY IN ADVANCE.

putt putt

HAVE FUN! WE'LL BE BACK IN TWO HOURS.

MARY POPP
JUNE

NOW, DO YOU ALL HAVE YOUR MONEY?

YUP.

YUP.

UHHHH.

NEXT?

EMMA? I TOLD YOU THREE TO MAKE SURE YOU BROUGHT YOUR MONEY.

I **DID**, BUT I CAN'T FIIIIIND IT.

MARY ANNE, I NEED YOUR HELP!
...IS THAT CRYING IN THE BACKGROUND?

YEAH, THE PHONE WOKE THE BABIES.
OH JEEZ, I'M SORRY. LISTEN, EMMA CAN'T FIND HER TICKET MONEY. WOULD YOU MIND...?
SURE THING. LET ME JUST QUIET THEM DOWN AND I'LL LOOK AROUND, OKAY?

SENIOR
STUDENT

ALL RIGHT, LET'S GO GO GO! WE'VE GOT A MINUTE UNTIL --

JUNIOR MINTS...
M&MS...
POPCOOOOORN.

YOU GUYS, WE DON'T HAVE TIME -- OR MONEY. AND ANYWAY, YOU JUST HAD LUNCH.
WE HAVE ROOM FOR A **SNACK.**
OUR MOMS GAVE US EXTRA MONEY FOR A **TREAT.**

WE NEED FOUR SEATS TOGETHER, WITH ONE ON THE AISLE FOR ASHLEY.
SHH!
SORRY.
SORRY.
whew

EVERYTHING WENT WELL UNTIL RIGHT NEAR THE END OF THE MOVIE.

WHOOPS.
tk tk tk

AACK!

WHAT--??
hee hee hee hee hee mmmph hee

THANK GOODNESS.

WHAT HAPPENED?
ASK HER.

WE WERE ON THE BALCONY AND --
snrrk
EMMA WAS EATING JUNIOR MINTS BUT --
I GOT SOMEONE ON THE HEAD!!
mmph

haha
haha

ahahaha

OH WELL.
I CAN ALWAYS SEE IT ON TV.

AS FOR ME, I NOW HAD MY WEDDING SHOES...

BUT STILL NO IDEA ABOUT A GIFT FOR MOM AND WATSON.

Thursday, June 25

Until today, I didn't know that "barber" is a dirty word. But it is - to little boys. Here's how I found out: When the mothers and fathers dropped their children off at Kristy's house this morning, they all looked guilty. It turned out that they'd decided the boys, except for baby Tony, needed their hair cut before the wedding. Since the barber is only open from 9:00 until 5:00, guess what they asked us poor, defenseless, unprepared baby-sitters to do? They asked us to take Luke, David Michael, Berk, Andrew, Peter, and Patrick to poor, defenseless, unprepared Mr. Gates, whose barbershop is just around the corner from the elementary school. When we told the boys about their field trip, all six of them turned pale, then red, and began throwing tantrums...

Mary Anne

CHAPTER 10

WEDDING COUNTDOWN: THURSDAY -- TWO DAYS TO GO
ALL RIGHT, TEAM.
WE'VE GOT SIX BOYS GETTING HAIRCUTS, AND EIGHT KIDS STAYING BEHIND. HOW SHOULD WE SPLIT UP? SHOULD THREE OF US GO TO THE BARBER?
THAT SEEMS LIKE TOO MANY.
MR. GATES HAS AN ASSISTANT, RIGHT? SO WE CAN GET TWO HAIRCUTS AT A TIME. THERE'LL ONLY BE FOUR TO WATCH.
GOOD POINT.
Kristy
OKAY. I'LL GO, SINCE I'M RELATED TO MOST OF THESE BOYS, AND I'LL TAKE ONE OF YOU WITH ME. ANY VOLUNTEERS?
I...I'LL GO.
I WOULDN'T MIND A BABY BREAK... I GUESS.
THEN LET'S CORRAL SOME KIDS.

BARBER TIME!
NO NO NO NO NO NO!
NOOOOOO!
WE'RE NOT COMING DOWN!
FINE!
OH MARY ANNE!
WOULD YOU GET NANNIE ON THE PHONE AND TELL HER TO COME OVER?
TELL HER THE BOYS ARE --
WAIT! WAAAAAIT!
Kristy

YOU WANT ME TO LOOK LIKE AN OWL, DON'T YOU.
THAT'S WHAT I LOOKED LIKE AFTER I WENT TO MR. GATES LAST TIME.

AND MY HAIR JUST GOT NORMAL AGAIN.
DAVID MICHAEL, DON'T YOU TRUST MOM? SHE DOESN'T WANT AN OWL AT HER WEDDING, EITHER, AND SHE CHOSE MR. GATES.

the sweet bean
STONEYBROOK BARBERSHOP
UUUUUUGH.

jingle
WELL, WHAT HAVE WE HERE?
ISN'T IT **OBVIOUS?**

HI, MR. GATES. MY MOM'S GETTING MARRIED ON SATURDAY, AND ALL THESE KIDS NEED HAIRCUTS.
BUT NOT TOO SHORT.
NOT OVER MY EARS.
NOT TOO LONG AT THE SIDES.
LEAVE MY PART ALONE.
I DON'T **WANT** A PART.
DO YOU HAVE LOLLIPOPS?
ONE AT A TIME, ONE AT A TIME.

THIS IS MR. PRATT, OUR OTHER BARBER. HE'LL BE HELPING ME TODAY.
H-HEY.

NOW, WHICH TWO OF YOU WOULD LIKE TO GO FIRST?
NOT ME!!

LUKE AND DAVID MICHAEL.
NO!!

I WILL CALL NANNIE.

I'M ROCKET MAN!
OH NO YOU AREN'T!

DON'T MAKE ME LOOK LIKE AN OWL.
NOW, NOW.

IT SEEMS I'VE GOT A BIG JAR OF LOLLIPOPS RIGHT OVER THERE. BUT I ONLY GIVE THEM TO MY **WELL-BEHAVED** CUSTOMERS.

I'M TOO OLD FOR LOLLIPOPS.
ME TOO.
(ASKED FOR TWO LAST TIME)

THAT DOES IT. MR. GATES?

EXCUSE US FOR A MOMENT.

YOU TWO ARE BEING JUST PLAIN RUDE. WHO TAUGHT YOU TO SPEAK THIS WAY TO ADULTS?
MY FRIENDS AND I **TRIED** TO MAKE THIS FUN FOR YOU, BUT YOU'RE TOO MUCH TO HANDLE.
I GUESS I'LL JUST HAVE TO CALL NANNIE, AFTER ALL, AND ASK HER TO TAKE OVER.
NO! NO, PLEASE!
WE'LL BE GOOD, I PROMISE!!

WE DID IT! SOMEHOW WE DID IT!
THANK GOODNESS.

NOW IF I COULD JUST THINK OF A WEDDING PRESENT FOR MOM AND WATSON, THIS WOULD BE A PERFECT DAY.
UH...

A TOASTER OVEN?
A ROLLING PIN?
A PICNIC BASKET?
HMM.

A FIRE ENGINE.
A ROBOT!
HEY, KRISTY?
sigh
DO I HAVE TO GET THEM A PRESENT, TOO?
IT WOULD BE NICE.
HELP ME THINK OF ONE.
OH, BROTHER.

Friday, June 26

Unfiar! Today it rained! All day!

I guess we baby sitters shouldnt complain to much since this was the first rainy day all weak. But still it was a yucky day wether wise. The kids were not to bad though.

Hey Kristy how come we have to write in the diary this weak? We're all sitting so we all know whats going on right? I guess its just the rules right? Anyway it cant hurt.

Anyway the morning went okay but by the time lunch was over we were running out of things to do then I got this really fun idea . . .

* Claudia *

CHAPTER 11

WEDDING COUNTDOWN: FRIDAY -- ONE DAY TO GO!
I'M BOOOORED.
I'M BORED I'M BORED I'M BORED!
MY LEG HUUUURTS.
GET **BACK** HERE!
MORBIDDA DESTINY...
WE'VE GOT TO DO SOMETHING -- **FAST!**
BUT WHAT? WE'VE DONE EVERYTHING ALREADY, THAT'S THE PROBLEM.
Berk
WE SHOULD PROBABLY SEPARATE THEM. THIS IS GETTING OUT OF HAND.
ALTHOUGH...

WHAT IF WE COULD THINK OF A PROJECT FOR THE WHOLE GROUP, THAT OUR SMALLER GROUPS COULD WORK ON SEPARATELY?
LIKE A SHOW?
EXACTLY.

HOW ABOUT A TALENT SHOW? EVEN THE LITTLEST KIDS COULD BE IN IT.
THAT MIGHT WORK!

WE ONLY HAVE TO KEEP THEM BUSY UNTIL ABOUT 4:00. THEN WE HAVE TO GET THEM DRESSED FOR THE REHEARSAL DINNER.
OH, THAT'S RIGHT! I ALMOST FORGOT.

WHEN MOM FIRST TOLD ME THE PLAN, I HAD TO ASK WHAT A REHEARSAL DINNER WAS.

IT TURNS OUT THAT ON THE DAY BEFORE THE WEDDING, EVERYONE WHO'S GOING TO BE IN IT GETS TOGETHER AND PRACTICES, JUST LIKE THEY'RE PUTTING ON A PLAY.

AFTERWARD, THEY GO OUT WITH THEIR FAMILIES AND A FEW SPECIAL FRIENDS FOR A NICE DINNER.

AND SINCE WE'LL BE WATCHING THE KIDS, THE WHOLE CLUB WAS INVITED!

ALL WE HAD TO DO WAS SURVIVE UNTIL THEN.

YOU KNOW, THAT GIVES ME AN IDEA. INSTEAD OF PUTTING ON AN ORDINARY SHOW OR PLAY...
HOW ABOUT WE PUT ON A WEDDING?

YOU MEAN MARRY OFF THE KIDS?
SURE. ALL THESE POOR KIDS HAVE **HEARD** ABOUT FOR THE LAST WEEK IS THE WEDDING. WE MIGHT AS WELL PREPARE THEM FOR THE REAL THING, RIGHT?
I **LOVE** IT.

KRISTY, DO YOU STILL HAVE YOUR OLD MAKE-BELIEVE CLOTHES?
ACTUALLY...

I'VE GOT EVEN **MORE** OF THEM.
OUR OTHER GRANDMA SENT OVER A HUGE BOX FOR US LAST YEAR.

WELL, WE JUST CHOSE OUR HAPPY COUPLE.

IT'S ME! ME AND DAVID MICHAEL!
BECAUSE WE'RE THE SAME HEIGHT.

WITH THAT SETTLED, WE FOUND VOLUNTEERS FOR THE OTHER PARTS OF THE WEDDING...

AND THEN DIVIDED INTO OUR GROUPS TO REHEARSE.

LADIES AND GENTLEMEN.

WE ARE GATHERED HERE TODAY TO JOIN THESE GUYS IN HOLY GUACAMOLE.
IF YOU THINK YOU'RE READY, YOU CAN TAKE THE OATH.

click
WE'RE READY.

KAREN, DO YOU PROMISE TO LOVE DAVID MICHAEL AND HELP HIM OUT AND NOT LET OLD BEN BREWER GET HIM?
I DO.
AND, DAVID MICHAEL, DO YOU PROMISE TO LOVE KAREN AND HELP HER OUT AND SHOW HER HOW TO RIDE A TWO-WHEELER?
I GUESS.
OKAY.
ALSO, IF YOU HAVE ANY KIDS, BE NICE TO THEM.
YEAH!
DON'T GIVE THEM ANY BEDTIMES.
AND DON'T YELL AT THEM IF THEY FORGET TO FEED THE DOG.
AND ONCE IN A WHILE, LET THEM HAVE A SNACK BEFORE DINNER.
ALL RIGHT.
YOU MAY NOW KISS THE BRIDE!
WHAT?!
EW, EW!!

CHAPTER 12

WEDDING COUNTDOWN:
FRIDAY EVENING -- HALF A DAY TO GO

AS SOON AS WE GOT KAREN AND DAVID MICHAEL CALMED DOWN, IT WAS TIME TO START DRESSING THE KIDS.

EVERYONE'S CLOTHES WERE IN LABELED BAGS, SO IT SHOULD HAVE BEEN EASY. BUT, OF COURSE...
HUH?
OH, DO YOU HAVE SOMEONE ELSE'S BAG?
NOPE.
Andrew
HEY, KRISTY! COULD YOU COME HERE?
JUST STAY WITH MALLORY FOR A MINUTE.

MARY ANNE? WHAT'S UP?
LOOK AT THIS.
Beth

I FOUND THOSE IN BETH'S BAG. AND THIS WAS IN TONY'S.
IT'S GOT TO BE ASHLEY'S -- IT'S TOO BIG FOR THE OTHER KIDS.
GUYS!!
Mary Anne

OKAY, EMMA MEINER, TELL YOUR COUSIN WHAT YOU JUST TOLD ME.
EMMA.
I SWITCHED THE CLOTHES.
WHAT?
J-JUST A FEW THINGS FROM EACH BAG.
EMMA!

Kristy

EMMA...
WHAT YOU DID WAS REALLY BAD. WE ONLY HAVE ONE HOUR UNTIL YOUR PARENTS COME TO PICK YOU UP. THEY EXPECT US -- ALL OF US -- TO BE DRESSED AND READY.

THANKS TO YOU, WE MIGHT NOT BE READY AT ALL.

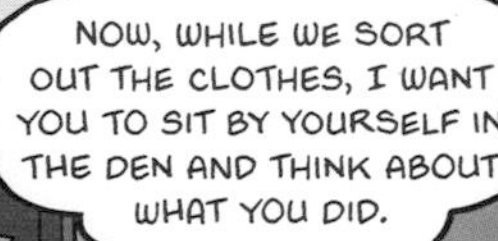
NOW, WHILE WE SORT OUT THE CLOTHES, I WANT YOU TO SIT BY YOURSELF IN THE DEN AND THINK ABOUT WHAT YOU DID.

IT TOOK HALF AN HOUR, BUT FINALLY...
WE WERE PRETTY SURE WE HAD EVERYTHING SORTED OUT.
AT 4:30, WE DIVIDED INTO GROUPS AGAIN, AND I LET EMMA OUT OF THE DEN.
I'm SORRY, KRISTY.
AND I'm SORRY I GOT MAD.
BUT PROMISE ME YOU WON'T DO ANYTHING ELSE NAUGHTY TODAY.
OR TOMORROW. WE ALL HAVE TO BE ON OUR BEST BEHAVIOR.
I PROMISE.

HEY!
HOW ABOUT A PICTURE?
BIG KIDS ON THE COUCH!
GRACE, PUT BETH IN YOUR LAP, OKAY?
HURRY, KRISTY! BEFORE THEY MOVE!

click!
OH, WHO'S **THIS** HANDSOME CROWD?!
WOULDN'T THIS MAKE A CUTE HOLIDAY CARD!!
WHAT'S BETH DOING WEARING TIGHTS?
heh

AND WITH THAT, THE AUNTS, UNCLES, AND FIELDINGS DROVE THEIR KIDS BACK TO WATSON'S, WHILE THE REST OF THE BABY-SITTERS CLUB LEFT SO THEY COULD GET DRESSED THEMSELVES.

JEEZ, THE HOUSE SEEMS KIND OF EMPTY NOW.
I'M GONNA MISS THOSE KIDS.
WE WON'T.

TICKLE THE FANCY BOY!
EEP!!

YOU KNOW...
DAVID MICHAEL MIGHT NOT MISS SHARING, BUT I BET HE'LL MISS HAVING KIDS HIS OWN AGE AROUND.

Hmm.
MAYBE HE AND KAREN WILL GET ALONG BETTER THAN I THINK.

I WON'T BOTHER YOU WITH TOO MANY DETAILS OF THE REHEARSAL.
ALL YOU NEED TO KNOW IS THAT IT WENT REASONABLY WELL, CONSIDERING WE WERE REHEARSING AN OUTDOOR WEDDING IN THE ALL-PURPOSE ROOM OF A CHURCH...
AND THAT WE HAD A MINOR CRISIS WHEN KAREN FOUND OUT THE FLORIST COULDN'T GET HER YELLOW ROSE PETALS, AND SHE'D HAVE TO MAKE DO WITH WHITE INSTEAD.
WHITE?!
WHAT'S WRONG WITH THAT?
EVIL WITCHES USE WHITE FLOWERS IN ALL THEIR MOST POWERFUL SPELLS. MORBIDDA DESTINY WILL BE ABLE TO SENSE THEM FROM NEXT DOOR.
SHE'LL TAKE THEM AND BECOME THE STRONGEST WITCH AND THEN --
BA-KOOM!!
AIEEEEEEE!!
WHAT?
NOTHING, NOTHING.
NOT ANOTHER WORD ABOUT MAGIC, KAREN.
NOT ONE.

AND THEN IT WAS TIME FOR THE REHEARSAL DINNER AT WATSON'S.

CLAUDIA HAD HELPED ME PICK OUT A NEW DRESS THE WEEK BEFORE, AND I FELT **VERY** GLAMOROUS.

WE KEPT THE KIDS POLITE DURING DINNER...

AND THEN WE HAD SOME TIME TO OURSELVES.

...THIS IS MY NEW ROOM.

I KNEW IT WAS GOING TO BE BIG, BUT I WASN'T EXPECTING **THIS.**
THINK OF THE SLUMBER PARTIES!
THINK OF WHAT YOU CAN **DO** WITH THE ROOM.
A MURAL... A CANOPY BED...
I DON'T KNOW HOW I FEEL ABOUT THIS VIEW, THOUGH.
AT LEAST IT'S NOT LOOKING INTO MORBIDDA DESTINY'S HOUSE.

THE HIGHLIGHT OF THE EVENING CAME AS THINGS WERE DRAWING TO A CLOSE.
GIRLS?

THAT'S YOUR PAY FOR A JOB **VERY** WELL DONE...
AND A LITTLE BONUS.
WE'RE RICH!!

WITH THAT, THE LAST DAY BEFORE THE WEDDING CAME TO AN END.
AND I STILL HAD NO IDEA OF WHAT TO GIVE MOM AND WATSON.

Thank you,
Kristy!
We love
you!

CHAPTER 13
WEDDING COUNTDOWN:
SATURDAY -- ZERO HOUR
grab!
YES!!

THE WEDDING WASN'T UNTIL TWO IN THE AFTERNOON, BUT THERE WAS A LOT TO DO BEFOREHAND.

MOM HAD TO PACK FOR HER HONEYMOON...

AND THEN NANNIE AND MOM HAD TO GO GET THEIR HAIR DONE.

WHEN THEY CAME BACK, NANNIE MADE US ALL EAT SOMETHING.
I'M TOO NERVOUS.

JUST A LITTLE SOMETHING.
NGUHHHH.
SHE REALLY **WAS** MOM'S MOM.

AFTER WE'D EATEN ENOUGH FOR NANNIE, IT WAS TIME TO GET DRESSED.
HEY, MARY ANNE! MARY ANNE!!
KRISTY?
YOU WANT TO HELP ME GET DRESSED?
SURE!

tok
tok
tok
WELL?

zip

KRISTY...

YOU LOOK **BEAUTIFUL!**

MY BOUQUET AND THE FLOWERS FOR MY HAIR HAD BEEN DELIVERED TO WATSON'S, SO I WAS AS DRESSED AS I COULD GET FOR THE TIME BEING.

SEE YOU AT THE WEDDING!

SINCE MOM AND WATSON COULDN'T SEE EACH OTHER BEFORE THE WEDDING, MOM, KAREN, AND I WENT INTO A SPARE ROOM, WHERE NANNIE PUT THE FINISHING TOUCHES ON US.

IT'S TIME.

YOU'RE NEXT, HONEY.

AIEEEE!

I, AH, BROUGHT SOMETHING FOR THE BRIDE AND GROOM.
OH! THANK YOU, MRS. PORTER.
DON'T **TAKE** IT! THE MAGICS!! THEY --

...
THANKS...

MRS. PORTER.

LATER, THE CATERER WHEELED OUT THE WEDDING CAKE, AND WE ALL GATHERED AROUND TO WATCH MOM AND WATSON CUT THE FIRST SLICE.

AT THAT MOMENT, I KNEW WHAT TO GIVE MOM AND MY STEPFATHER.

THANK YOU, KRISTY.

YOU DID GREAT.

REMEMBER, JUST CALL IF YOU NEED ANYTHING.
THANKS, NANNIE. BUT I CAN TAKE CARE OF THESE KIDS NO PROBLEM.
WE'LL SEE ABOUT THAT.

ALL RIGHT, CHAMPS, YOU HEARD MOM. I'M IN CHARGE WHILE THEY'RE ON THEIR HONEYMOON.
SO HERE ARE THE HOUSE RULES.
uuugh
ONE. DINNER EVERY NIGHT WILL BE PIZZA.
TWO. EVERYONE MUST GO TO BED AN HOUR LATER THAN USUAL.
THREE. NO EATING IN THE KITCHEN. FOOD IS ONLY ALLOWED BY THE TV, AND IT MUST BE ON.
DAVID MICHAEL, YOU CANNOT MISS A SINGLE CARTOON.
DO I STILL HAVE TO TAKE MY VITAMINS?
YES. DON'T PRESS YOUR LUCK.
ha ha ha ha ha

WITH THAT SETTLED, IT WAS TIME FOR ME TO START WORKING ON MOM AND WATSON'S PRESENT.
EVENTUALLY I'D NEED CLAUDIA'S HELP, BUT I MIGHT AS WELL GET MY THOUGHTS TOGETHER BEFORE TALKING TO HER ABOUT IT.

I DID A LITTLE RESEARCH IN MOM'S OFFICE...

AND I DOODLED FOR A BIT TO GET MY IDEAS DOWN.
BSC

HEY, KRISTY?
YEAH?

I KNOW WHAT I'M GIVING MOM AND WATSON.
WHAT'S THAT?

A GOLDFISH.
AND THAT'S EXACTLY WHAT HE DID.

THE NEXT DAY, I WENT OVER TO CLAUDIA'S EARLY SO I COULD TALK TO HER ABOUT MY IDEA BEFORE THE MEETING.
HERE'S WHAT I HAVE SO FAR.

I WANT IT TO SHOW BOTH FAMILIES, AND HOW THEY BECOME ONE -- SOMETHING LIKE THIS.
BUT I NEED HELP WITH THE DESIGN.

COULD YOU SHOW ME HOW TO DRAW A BOW, AND THE LITTLE FLOWERS YOU DREW ON THAT ART PROJECT FOR MR. FINEMAN LAST YEAR?
OR YOU COULD USE A **REAL** BOW. HANG ON.

LET'S SEE WHAT WE'VE GOT!

OKAY, LET'S DO SOME SIMPLE ROSES. WE'RE GOING TO USE A PENCIL TO SKETCH.

GOT IT.

① First, lightly draw a circle.

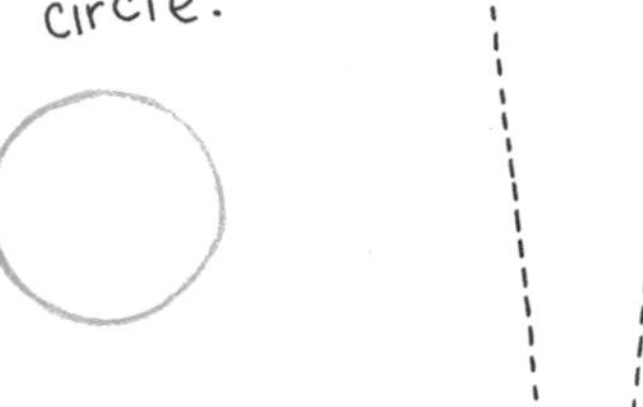

② Then make curvy lines inside, working toward the middle.

③ And draw puffy bits around it!

NOW ALL YOU HAVE TO DO IS TRACE OVER IT IN PEN AND ERASE THE PENCIL MARKS.

OH, THAT'S LOVELY!
CLAUDIA'S A GOOD TEACHER.
LOOK WHAT I'VE GOT.
MOM GOT THE PHOTOS SHE TOOK AT THE WEDDING PRINTED!
OHHHHH!!

THERE YOU ARE, GETTING READY TO WALK UP THE AISLE.
OH, AND YOU'RE WALKING IN THIS ONE! YOU LOOK SO NERVOUS.
I THOUGHT I WAS GOING TO TRIP.
AW, THERE'S KAREN AND ANDREW. THEY'RE SO CUTE.
AND YOUR MOM AND WATSON KISSING!
I CAN'T BELIEVE YOU TOOK A PICTURE OF **THAT!!**

AND HERE'S MOM AND WATSON CUTTING THE CAKE.
THAT'S THE MOMENT THAT GAVE ME THE IDEA FOR MOM AND WATSON'S WEDDING PRESENT.
WHAT IS?
WHEN THEIR HANDS CAME TOGETHER, I STARTED THINKING ABOUT HOW WE CAME TOGETHER, TOO.
HOW WE ALL MAKE ONE BIG FAMILY NOW. AND...
I WANTED TO SHOW THAT.
SO CLAUDIA'S BEEN HELPING ME PUT THIS TOGETHER.
KRISTY, THAT'S REALLY SOMETHING.
YEAH. I THINK IT'LL MEAN A LOT TO YOUR MOM.

??
EVERYONE COMING TOGETHER TO MAKE A NEW FAMILY.
THAT'S WHAT THE WEDDING HAD BEEN ALL ABOUT.

Karen
Andrew
Watson
Elizabeth
Charlie
Sam
Kristy
David Michael

ANN M. MARTIN'S The Baby-sitters Club is one of the most popular series in the history of publishing — with more than 190 million books in print worldwide — and inspired a generation of young readers. Her novels include *Belle Teal, A Corner of the Universe* (a Newbery Honor book), *Here Today, A Dog's Life,* and *On Christmas Eve,* as well as the much-loved collaborations, *P.S. Longer Letter Later* and *Snail Mail No More,* with Paula Danziger, and *The Doll People* and *The Meanest Doll in the World,* written with Laura Godwin and illustrated by Brian Selznick. She lives in upstate New York.

GALE GALLIGAN is the creator of the *New York Times* bestselling Baby-sitters Club graphic novel adaptations of *Dawn and the Impossible Three, Kristy's Big Day, Boy-Crazy Stacey,* and *Logan Likes Mary Anne!* by Ann M. Martin. They are also the creator of *Freestyle,* an original graphic novel that they both wrote and illustrated. Gale was featured in The *Claudia Kishi Club,* a documentary now streaming on Netflix. When they aren't making comics, Gale enjoys knitting, reading, and spending time with their family and adorable pet rabbits. They live in Pearl River, New York. Visit them online at galesaur.com.

DON'T MISS THE OTHER BABY-SITTERS CLUB GRAPHIC NOVELS!